DIRTY ROTTEN SCOUNDREL

A J.J. GRAVES MYSTERY (BOOK 3)

LILIANA HART

DIRTY ROTTEN SCOUNDREL

NEW YORK TIMES BESTSELLING AUTHOR

LILIANA HART

To Scott,

I could never repay you for your absolute love and support.
Except maybe with ice cream. I love you, always.

OTHER BOOKS

The MacKenzies of Montana
Dane's Return
Thomas's Vow
Riley's Sanctuary
Cooper's Promise
Grant's Christmas Wish
The MacKenzies Boxset

MacKenzie Security Series
Seduction and Sapphires
Shadows and Silk
Secrets and Satin
Sins and Scarlet Lace
Sizzle
Crave
Trouble Maker
Scorch
MacKenzie Security Omnibus 1
MacKenzie Security Omnibus 2

Lawmen of Surrender (MacKenzies-1001 Dark Nights)
1001 Dark Nights: Captured in Surrender
1001 Dark Nights: The Promise of Surrender
Sweet Surrender
Dawn of Surrender

The MacKenzie World (read in any order)
Trouble Maker
Bullet Proof
Deep Trouble
Delta Rescue
Desire and Ice
Rush
Spies and Stilettos
Wicked Hot
Hot Witness
Avenged
Never Surrender

JJ Graves Mystery Series
Dirty Little Secrets
A Dirty Shame
Dirty Rotten Scoundrel
Down and Dirty
Dirty Deeds
Dirty Laundry
Dirty Money

Addison Holmes Mystery Series
Whiskey Rebellion
Whiskey Sour
Whiskey For Breakfast
Whiskey, You're The Devil

Whiskey on the Rocks
Whiskey Tango Foxtrot
Whiskey and Gunpowder

The Gravediggers
The Darkest Corner
Gone to Dust
Say No More

Stand Alone Titles
Breath of Fire
Kill Shot
Catch Me If You Can
All About Eve
Paradise Disguised
Island Home
The Witching Hour

Books by Liliana Hart and Scott Silverii
The Harley and Davidson Mystery Series
The Farmer's Slaughter
A Tisket a Casket
I Saw Mommy Killing Santa Claus
Get Your Murder Running
Deceased and Desist
Malice In Wonderland
Tequila Mockingbird
Gone With the Sin

ACKNOWLEDGMENTS

To the countless number of law enforcement officers, morticians, and medical examiners who let me pick their brains while I'm researching a book. They are truly at the top of their fields and true heroes. Any mistakes made in the book are mine and mine alone.

PROLOGUE

I'D NEVER GIVEN THE PHRASE *DEAD MAN WALKING* MUCH thought. Not until a few hours ago when I'd been faced with the ghost of my father. Only he hadn't been a ghost. He'd been flesh and blood and bone—and he'd been breathing.

Only a few short hours ago, I realized I was happy for the first time in as long as I could remember—I had a career I hadn't planned on and wasn't overly fond of, but it paid most of my bills. And I had a man who loved me despite my numerous flaws. I should have known it wouldn't last. Anyone with the last name Graves was cursed from the cradle.

The memories of the afternoon run in with my father looped over and over in my mind. Jack had dropped me off at the house I'd grown up in—an old Victorian that backed up to the Potomac River. It was a house that brought nothing but bad memories—of a childhood filled with neglect, as well as the death of an old lover that had spattered the walls with crimson. The house was going on the market, and then it would be another family's burden—an empty vessel to fill with their own memories.

I'd waved goodbye to Jack and had every intention of packing the last of my things. I'd barely had the door closed at my back when I realized I wasn't alone. Fear overwhelmed me. I'd experienced it before and the memories of death were still too fresh in my mind.

The floorboards creaked as he came from one of the back rooms and I froze in terror.

"So you've decided to move in with Jack," he said. "I wondered how long it would take the two of you to stop dancing and get down to business. I always did like that boy."

I tripped over my feet and slammed back against the door. Mewling whimpers escaped from my throat as my sweaty hand fumbled for the doorknob. But then the familiarity of that voice caught up to my brain and my knees turned to jelly.

"What's wrong, Jaye? Aren't you going to say hello?"

"Dad?" My legs gave out completely and I slid to the floor.

He smiled like he hadn't just destroyed my world and stuck his hands in the pockets of his khakis. All I could think was he looked good for a dead man—I'd know since I'd seen more than my fair share.

He was thinner than the last time I'd seen him, the lines in his face a little deeper. He skimmed just under six feet and his hair was thick and the color of a deer pelt. His eyes were hazel and he still wore the same tortoise shell glasses he always had. He looked more like a college professor than a mortician or a criminal, but that was probably the point. My dad could be accused of being a lot of things but an idiot wasn't one of them. He knew how to blend—how to fade into the background. Which was one of the reasons I'd never bought that he and my mom drove over the cliff on purpose during a fight. It was too big of a splash. If they were going to commit double suicide they would've popped a couple of cyanide pills in the privacy of their own home.

I shook my head, trying to get my thoughts back together, and I realized he was speaking to me.

He sighed and squatted down beside me. I tried to crawl backwards, but the wood was solid at my back. "You always did like to overdramatize things. Emotions only get in the way of the important things in life. We taught you to keep a clear head, no matter what the circumstance."

"Some things can be taught. Others are passed through the blood." I met his gaze with all the anger I'd been holding inside since I'd found out I hadn't really been theirs. "I guess you failed on both accounts there."

His surprise at my knowledge was quickly masked. "You've always been ours. We loved you the same. The how you came to be here is just all in the details."

I knew the signs of shock. I was a doctor, for God's sake. My pulse was rapid and my skin cold and clammy with sweat. My pulse raced and I knew if I looked in the mirror my eyes would be dilated to the point that only a thin ring of gray would be showing.

"Since you know about your birth, I'm going to assume you found the boxes of papers in the bunker. The body was still there the last time I checked, so I know it wasn't the FBI. I need those boxes, Jericho."

A sound I didn't recognize escaped my mouth and tears I couldn't control dripped down my cheeks and onto my shirt. My father was the only person who ever used my real name, but even then it was only when I was in trouble. There were only a handful of people who even knew what my name was because I loathed it with a flaming hot passion. It didn't bode well that he was using it now.

His hand came up and I stopped breathing when his finger trailed down my cheek, following the path of my tears. I knew what it was like to have the air cut off, so oxygen couldn't reach the lungs no matter how hard you tried or struggled. I knew what it was like to gasp and claw your way toward death. I'd been there. And feeling the touch of a dead man, which proved he wasn't really dead after all, brought an onslaught of memories I'd tried hard to forget over the last months.

Breathe, Jaye. I had to remind myself to suck in oxygen, just like I had after I'd been attacked by Jeremy Mooney—a sociopath who'd taken three other lives before he'd decided to add me to his collection. I felt the airway of my throat open and I sucked in a gulping breath.

My dad took my chin between his thumb and forefinger and turned my head so I had no choice but to look straight at him. "I've been through the house from top to bottom and the boxes aren't here. You haven't stepped foot inside for months, so it's been a good place for me to lay low."

"I ccc—couldn't—"

I wanted to scream. To tell him how much I hated the house and everything it represented. All the lies. And I hated the fact that this had been the place I'd almost died—only a dozen or so feet from where I sat now.

"I know what happened here." He didn't explain how or why he knew. "It's best you haven't been around. The Feds still have the house under surveillance. They were never really looking at you anyway."

I jerked at that bit of knowledge. I hadn't noticed anyone hanging around, federal or otherwise, for almost a year. It made me wonder if Jack knew. There wasn't much that got by him.

"Could've fooled me," I croaked out. I'd been an emergency room doctor at Augusta General when my parents had taken that drive over the cliff. The FBI had questioned me for weeks and they'd dogged my every step. If I hadn't quit my job when I had I probably would've been fired. "Wh—who is the body?"

He looked at his watch and then back at me, his gaze determined and a little bit sorry. "A mistake. Now tell me where the boxes are. I'm assuming either with Jack or at the funeral home. I haven't been able to search either location and time is running out."

We both heard it at the same time. The sound of tires on the graveled road coming to a stop. My dad sighed and quirked the corner of his mouth in a smile. "I guess we'll have to do this later. We'll talk again soon."

I watched as he walked down the darkened hallway and disappeared right in front of my eyes. I'd almost convinced myself that I'd been hallucinating—that the horrible memories of the house had somehow manifested into my own reality. But then I looked down at my hand and realized I held a circle of silver, the outside of the wide band engraved with a complicated design.

It sat like molten lead in my palm and I almost dropped it. The last time I'd seen the ring it had been on my mother's finger.

Not a hallucination.

1

My name is J.J. Graves and I'm the coroner for King George County, Virginia. Since there isn't a huge demand for coroners in a county that has a population of just over twenty thousand, I supplement my meager income through Graves Funeral Home, working for those who meet death the natural way.

I live in Bloody Mary—one of the four towns that makes up King George County—and despite the rather macabre name, most people manage to make a good life and live the American dream. I preferred not to dream. I'd found my dreams turned to nightmares much too easily. I'm fourth generation mortician. First generation law-abiding citizen. And either way, it's a hell of a legacy.

Three A.M. had come and gone, but I had yet to close my eyes. Slivers of moonlight managed to find their way between the cracks and gnarls of tree limbs and shone into the floor-to-ceiling windows that took up an entire wall. The ceiling fan whirred overhead and I stared at it with utter concentration, hoping the repetitiveness would lull me to sleep. My eyes felt like they were weighted with sand, but every time I closed them I could see his face—my father's—and I could feel the icy touch of his finger as it trailed down my cheek.

I hunkered farther into the mattress and pulled the down comforter up to my chin. I'd been chilled for hours and nothing could warm me. Not even Jack, who slept in peaceful ignorance beside me.

My life had changed irrevocably in the past couple of weeks. I'd somehow found myself living with the man I'd called my best friend since childhood. Our bond was solid—unbreakable even—and we had a lifetime of knowing and loving each other to anchor us. But that was before my dead father made an appearance.

The strength of our relationship was bound to be tested, and I could admit the reason I hadn't found the courage to tell Jack about my father was that I was afraid it would be the excuse he'd need to walk away. I still didn't understand why he loved me—why I deserved that love—and I kept waiting for him to tell me he'd changed his mind. That it had all been a terrible misunderstanding.

Jack believed in law and order, and as sheriff of King George County, he was elected to the office with those principles firmly in place. He was already skating on thin ice with the upcoming election because of his relationship with me. Sins of the fathers and all that nonsense. My father showing up now, of all times, would just add nails to the coffin. It was safe to say that my father had never met law and order.

The burning sensation in my gut was either an ulcer or the knowledge that I might not be the best thing for Jack, even though I knew with certainty he was the best thing that could ever happen to me. And the thought flitted through my mind, not for the first time, that maybe I should be the one to walk away. For his own good.

I shivered beneath the covers and figured I might as well get up and start coffee. I didn't have any dead to deal with at the moment, but I had unpacking to do. It was pitiful how few belongings I had to bring with me into my new life with Jack.

"Are you going to tell me what's bothering you?" Jack asked, his voice husky with sleep. He rolled so he faced me and pulled me close against his body. He hissed out a breath when the ice of my skin made contact, but he didn't let go. He just pulled the covers tighter around us and cocooned me with his warmth. "You're thinking so loud that neither one of us is going to get much sleep if you don't shut down."

"I've just got a lot on my mind." I couldn't tell him. I was ashamed of where I'd come from. Afraid that Jack would be ashamed of me. And I wasn't sure that was something I could face. "Can't turn my brain off."

I felt him tense behind me and he turned me so we were face to face. Jack liked to meet problems head on. I'd had enough problems in my life that I didn't mind avoiding them whenever possible.

"Are you having regrets?" His touch was gentle as he brushed the hair back from my face, but I could see the tension in his jaw—the worry in his eyes. I realized he was talking about us.

"No, of course not." I leaned in and kissed him on the base of the jaw, his morning whiskers prickly against my skin. "I never could. You're the best thing that's ever happened to me.

I have no regrets about moving in with you, about sharing a home with you."

His hand massaged the back of my neck and down to the tight muscles between my shoulder blades. "I should have gone with you inside the house. It wasn't something you needed to face on your own. You've been upset ever since."

I licked my lips and snuggled closer so I wouldn't have to look him in the eyes when I lied. "It hit me harder than I thought it would. I'll just be glad to get rid of it once and for all."

"That's fine. But I want to make sure you really feel like this is home and that you're comfortable here. If you want to make changes to a room or buy new furniture just tell me."

My lips twitched at the thought of spending time and money decorating a house that was already beautiful. I'd never been a typical girl growing up—just one of the boys playing sandlot baseball, building forts, and tromping through the woods. And then I'd gone on to medical school and my residency and I'd been so tired from lack of sleep that thinking of fixing my hair or putting on makeup and a nice outfit to attract the opposite sex had been the farthest thing from my mind.

"I don't think I'm going to be very good at living together," I said softly.

"You're naked and in my bed. I think you're doing a pretty damned good job so far."

I rolled my eyes, but he couldn't see it. "I mean I've never lived with anyone before. I don't know how to cook or decorate for holidays, and I never remember to put seasonal wreaths on the door like every other woman in town."

"Thank God for that," Jack said dryly. "I've never been overly fond of seasonal wreaths."

I smacked him in the arm. "I'm just saying I've spent most of my life focused on my career. I don't want you to have these expectations and then have you disappointed when I don't meet them."

"Jaye, I've known you since we were barely walking. I know you can't cook. Just like I know you have a competitive streak a mile long and you can gut a fish with a precision that makes me jealous. We both have our strengths. It'll all work out okay."

We lay wrapped in each other a few minutes—soft touches and comfort. "I've decided to put in for vacation time," Jack said. "I have more days accumulated than I know what to do with, and I've got good men to cover for me."

I pulled back in surprise. "What? Why? You'll be bored out of your mind in a week."

He sighed and rubbed slow, soothing circles on my back. "You know we have to go back and look. To see if the body is still there. And anyway, we've got to report it to the authorities whether the body is still there or not. It's the right thing to do. The investigation will take some time, and it'll also make your parents' crimes and their deaths fresh again. I don't want you to have to handle it all by yourself."

In a moment of weakness I'd told Jack about the body I'd found in my parents' bunker behind their house in the

Poconos. The same body my father had so casually called a *mistake.*

I shook my head because I couldn't speak. I didn't want to go back there. I wanted to pretend I'd never found the body or taken the boxes my father was looking for. I wanted to pretend I wasn't J.J. Graves, mortician of the damned. I wanted to start my life with Jack and live with the illusion we were white picket fence kind of people. But I couldn't, and we weren't.

"You know we have to, Jaye. It'll haunt you forever if you don't see it through. We need to bury the past before we can move to the future."

I tried to swallow the lump in my throat. The past was far from buried and it made the future impossible.

"And after we get that taken care of, maybe we could make this arrangement more permanent."

I tried to laugh it off, but it came out as a nervous croak. My blood ran cold and my skin went clammy. I had a feeling I knew what he was going to say—he'd hinted at it a time or two—but I wasn't sure I was ready to hear it.

"It seems to me that we've got here is pretty permanent."

"I want to marry you, Jaye. I want to be a family. For it to be binding and permanent. I think after everything we've been through together that we both need that. I need it. I want you to be my wife."

I felt the constriction in my lungs and realized I wasn't breathing. And this time when I told myself to breathe my brain didn't listen.

"Jesus, Jaye. I'm not asking you to join a cult or commit murder. Breathe before you pass out."

I sucked in a deep breath and felt the tightness loosen in my chest. "I'm fine. I'm good," I wheezed out. "You just took me by surprise." The exasperation on his face was plain to see, and it reminded me of a similar look I'd seen from my father just hours before.

"I love you. And unless something has changed you love me too. This is just the natural progression of things. I've never said I love you to a woman before. Never wanted to spend my life with anyone or even think about marriage. Not until you."

My heart did a long, liquid roll inside my chest and I sighed at the sweetness and sincerity of his words. I knew he spoke the truth. I didn't want the magic of the moment to end between us, and I tried not to think about the future—about the possibility of Jack changing his mind once I told him the truth. But for now I could enjoy the fantasy—and be loved just a little.

"I'll marry you," I said, hoarsely.

I felt his relief and saw the quick flash of his smile. "I was hoping you'd say that. I didn't want to have to resort to torture techniques." Jack rolled us so I was on my back and he leaned over me, and the hardness nudging my thigh gave me a good idea what he had in mind.

My eyebrows raised at the feel of him. "It feels pretty torturous to me."

He cracked out a laugh and I couldn't help but grin, shifting beneath him so he fit more comfortably between my thighs, my ankles curling easily over his calves. I explored his skin with my hands—over taut muscles and scars, up his chest where the coarse chest hair curled around my fingers, and across the flat discs of his nipples that went rigid beneath my touch.

"God, you're pretty." I cupped his face with my hand and watched the uncomfortable embarrassment flash across his features. He looked like a man more suited to making action movies in Hollywood instead of reigning herd on citizens in bumfuck Virginia.

He had a chiseled, angular face and sensuous lips that constantly distracted me. His eyes were so dark they were almost black and thick brows winged above them. A thin scar slashed through his right eyebrow, giving him a somewhat disreputable appearance. And since it had been my cleat that had connected with his face while I'd been sliding into home, the mark made me feel somewhat sentimental. His hair was dark and cut close to his scalp, and over the last year or so his beard had become flecked with the occasional strand of silver.

"Flattery will get you everywhere," he grinned. "And since you've decided not to tell me what's bothering you, maybe I should go ahead and show you my interrogation techniques."

I gasped as his hand cupped my breast at the same moment he slid deep inside me. My legs came up to tighten around his waist and my blood pumped with excitement. My nails dug into his shoulders at the abrupt invasion, and Jack held still as he waited for me to adjust to the intrusion. I was morning soft, but hardly prepared to take something of Jack's size without a little preparation first.

He kissed me then, his teeth nipping at my bottom lip so he

could drink in my sighs. His tongue danced with mine, stroking, soothing, until I'd relaxed beneath him and my hips began to lift on their own, meeting his as he began to move in long, slow strokes.

My hands roamed down his back and his buttocks, feeling the muscles bunch beneath my fingers and the dampness of sweat on his flesh. Soft sighs and the rustle of sheets filled the air and my skin tingled as I felt the beginnings of an orgasm gathering deep inside of me. Jack always knew just where to touch—where to kiss—to make me go liquid beneath him.

The climax rolled through me like a wave and I shuddered beneath him as he took me higher and higher, prolonging the sensations until I wasn't sure I'd survive it.

"I can't—"

My hands slid limply from his back and to the mattress and my breath labored while my heart thudded in my chest. I felt Jack's heart beating against my breast—the same thumping rhythm in perfect sync with my own.

"Yes, you can," he whispered against my ear.

He stopped moving, kissing me softly as I continued to spasm around him. He was still hard inside of me and I shifted a little, watching his jaw clench as he tried to stay in control. Thoughts of exhaustion evaporated and I felt the need surge inside me once again. I was insatiable. But only with Jack. It had never been that way with anyone before, and I knew there could never be anyone after.

"My turn," I said, pushing against him so he rolled onto his back and straddling him. The angle was different—sharper—

deeper—and I sucked in a breath as he hit a spot that made my eyes cross.

"Jesus, Jack."

A laugh rumbled in his chest and was choked off when I tightened around him. "God, I love it when you do that."

I placed my hands on his chest and did it again. "I know. I try to stay in shape. Exercise is important."

"Mmm, I definitely know which of your muscles is my favorite." Perspiration dotted his brow, and I could tell he was close but trying to hold off. There was nothing I liked more than watching him lose control. It so rarely happened. And I loved knowing I was the one who could make him. He flexed inside me and I lost concentration for a moment. But this time wasn't about me. It was about Jack and the power we wielded over each other.

"Speaking of muscles," I said. And then I began to ride, fast and furious as his fingers bit into my hips. My eyes never left his and I watched as the dark brown bled to black the closer he came to fulfillment. And then I was just as lost as he was as we went over the edge together.

I collapsed onto his chest and snuggled against him as his arms came around me. My eyes drifted shut and contentment washed through me. I felt the weight of the covers as he pulled them over us and he rolled so we lay on our sides, our bodies still joined. His breath fluttered across my ear.

"Just think of all the years we wasted not doing this."

I grunted and wasn't sure I was capable of speech. My leg was thrown over his hip and I was still having aftershocks of what had to be one of the most incredible orgasms I'd ever experienced.

"Maybe so," I finally managed. "But I can't say I'm disappointed you had all that practice in the meantime." His laughter rumbled beneath my ear and I smiled.

"Sleep, love. I'll hold on to you."

That was all it took for me to drift off.

————

I HADN'T BEEN ASLEEP LONG when my phone rang. My head jerked up and hit Jack's chin, and he swore as we tried to untangle ourselves from the covers. I rubbed the top of my head and looked at the clock as I crawled across to the nightstand.

"Shit, it's barely five." A call coming in at that time could only mean one thing—someone had died.

"Dr. Graves," I answered.

"This is dispatch." I recognized Barbara Blanton's nasal voice without her having to tell me who she was. Barbara had been the dispatch operator for King George County since before I was born. "We've got a body over in Caledon State Park near Jones Pond. Police are already on the scene. You're up to bat, Doc Graves." She hung up the phone and I was already scrambling out of bed.

I had to figure there weren't a lot of dispatch operators like Barbara—at least I hoped not. I knew as soon as she hung up she'd dial her sister to let her know what had happened. It was impossible to keep secrets in a community of this size.

By dinner, everyone would know just as much as the police did.

"She said the police were already on site," I told Jack as I ran into the bathroom and turned on the shower. "Why didn't you get a call?"

"Colburn is on call tonight." Jack followed me into the bathroom and got towels out of the cabinet. I never remembered to get a towel until I was out of the shower and dripping all over the floor. "Besides, I already put in for that vacation time I was telling you about."

I stopped with one foot in the big, walk-in shower and narrowed my eyes at Jack. "Pretty damned cocky of you to assume I'd say yes." His gaze was steady, but I could see the humor lurking in his eyes and around the corners of his mouth.

"I was SWAT for a lot of years, sweetheart. Cocky is my middle name." He got into the shower behind me and closed the glass door, adjusting the showerhead for his height while I stood there with my mouth open.

Jack was already dressed by the time I came out of the bathroom. I had a towel wrapped around me and my hair dripped onto my shoulders.

"I'll make coffee," he said, looking up, his eyes going heavy lidded with arousal as he took in the sight of me. "Maybe we should just stop by the courthouse this afternoon and get the marriage license. Unless you want a big wedding."

My back stiffened and that sense of panic started to creep up my skin, rendering me cold. And angry. "Don't push it, Jack.

I said I'd marry you, but I'm not going to be rushed into anything. Weddings take time to plan."

"And long engagements would give you plenty of time to think of all the reasons you're too afraid to make a commitment and to live again."

I jerked back as if I'd been slapped and I felt the blood drain from my face.

"I'll meet you downstairs."

He left the room and I tried to focus on the present—on the body that waited for me—but there were too many other thoughts jumbled in my mind. My dad, the boxes he wanted so badly, the dead body I'd found in the Poconos, marrying Jack, and wondering what would happen if we got married and then he decided he couldn't handle all the baggage I brought with me. There was fear inside me. I knew Jack was right. But that didn't make the words hurt any less.

I dug in the drawer for clean underwear and a bra and then found a pair of jeans folded in a box of my clothes. The weather was still cool in the mornings, so I shoved my head and arms into a white T-shirt and pulled a gray long-sleeved Henley on top of it. I put white athletic socks on my feet and stepped into my worn hiking boots.

I didn't waste a lot of time looking in the mirror. My black hair was short—chin length—and it would be dry by the time I reached the scene. I hardly ever bothered with makeup, mostly because I didn't think of it. My face was angular—my cheekbones sharp and my chin slightly pointed. My eyes were big and gray and long lashed—a feature I now knew came from someone other than the people I'd called my parents—and the emotions swirling in them couldn't be hidden. I was scared. And it showed.

I grabbed a windbreaker from the closet just in case I got cold and jogged down the stairs. The smell of coffee hit me full force and Jack had a to-go cup ready to put in my hand. His weapon and badge weren't attached to his belt like normal, and the sight of him without them confused me for a moment before I remembered he was on vacation. But it was obvious he still planned to go with me to the crime scene.

My Suburban was parked in Jack's driveway, just like it had been every night for the last several weeks. Jack and I had been fueling the gossip mill for a while now, and if we went onto the scene with our current moods, we'd be fueling it even more.

I'd had the Suburban outfitted especially to haul bodies and my equipment. There were no back seats, just a flat bed and a hidden compartment beneath for my medical bag, camera, extra blankets, and a coverall.

Jack got in the passenger side without saying a word and I took a deep breath before I got in and started the engine. My hands gripped the wheel and I stared straight ahead, trying to get my thoughts in order. I felt Jack's gaze after a minute or two, but I didn't look at him.

"You know I love you," I finally said. "And I want to marry you."

I felt more than heard his sigh of relief. "Then what's the problem?"

"I'm afraid you'll eventually realize you made a mistake. And then I'll have to kill you for breaking my heart."

"With a promise like that, you can see why I'm crazy about you." His hand came up and rested on the back of my neck, squeezing at the tension that was sure to bring me a headache before the end of the day.

"I can see you're crazy period. I mean it, Jack. This thing with my parents—the mess they've left behind. It's not going to go away easily or quickly. It's something people are going to talk about until we're old and gray. It's something that will follow around our children and grandchildren."

"I like the idea of having children with you. Especially the part where we make them."

The temperature was getting very warm in the car and I flicked on the air conditioner to full blast.

"I'm serious. You have to decide if it's really worth it. It could cost you the election."

His hand froze on the back of my neck and I winced, as his grip got tighter. "You've got to be fucking kidding me. You think I give a shit about an election? You think it means more to me than you do?"

"I know you love being a cop. That you live and breathe it. I don't want to be the reason you can't be who you were meant to be."

"That's just bullshit, Jaye. I can be a cop anywhere. I've got enough experience to take any job I want. Believe me, I get offers all the time. And if you're worried about our children and the whispers that might follow them around then we can say to hell with Bloody Mary and find some place else to live. We're not tied here unless we want to be. My family will always be here when we need them, but my home will always be wherever you are."

I felt the tears threaten to fall and blinked rapidly to hold them back. I wanted to tell him about my dad. *Needed* to tell him. But I couldn't get the words past my frozen vocal cords.

"It's okay, Jaye. Whenever you're ready. Whatever it is we'll deal with it."

Jack knew me better than anyone else, and I knew he was referring to the secret I was keeping from him. I felt my muscles relax under his reassurance, and I promised myself I'd lay it all out for him soon.

I put the Suburban in reverse. "Let's go look at a body."

"It's a hell of a way to start a vacation."

2
―――――

CALEDON STATE PARK WAS A NATURAL RESERVE ALONG THE
uppermost edge of King George County. It backed up to the
Potomac River and it was a good place for camping and fish-
ing, and for boy scouts and school children to spend time
learning about nature.

Two police cars blocked the entrance to the park and I pulled
to a stop so whoever had guard duty could check me out.
Officer Martinez carried his flashlight in his left hand and had
his right resting on his weapon as he walked up to the Suburban. I'd worked with Martinez before and knew he was a
solid cop.

"Doc Graves," Martinez said when I rolled down the window,
and then he turned his gaze to Jack. "Hey, Sheriff. I thought
you were on vacation?"

Martinez was only a couple inches taller than me, putting him
around 5'10". His dark hair was cut stylishly and his face was
shaved smooth. He was one of Jack's recent hires to the
department, and it hadn't taken long for the word to get out

that he was single. When he smiled, a dimple peeked out on his cheek and his eyes lit up with good humor.

"I am," Jack replied. "I'm just here to help move the body."

"You guys are weird. If it were me on vacation I'd be soaking up the sun on some tropical island, surrounded by smokin' hot babes in bikinis who would bring me beer and rub my back with suntan lotion."

"Given it a lot of thought, have you?" Jack asked dryly.

Martinez grinned unrepentantly. "It's been a long winter, Sheriff."

"What've we got?" I asked before things could go too off course. "Some poor camper keel over from a heart attack?"

"Nope." Martinez shook his head. "A DB washed up on shore. Colburn is working it as homicide since the vic's face is missing. I'll let you see for yourself."

My eyebrows rose almost to my hairline at the thought of a victim not having a face. "Can't wait to see this one."

"I'm pretty sure you're the only woman I know who would ever say that, Doc Graves." Martinez got back in his squad car and backed up so I could get by, and I turned on my high beams as we rumbled over the rutted road that led into the preserve.

"Christ, why can't people just die in their sleep anymore?"

"Selfish bastards," Jack said, making me grin.

Tree limbs scraped the top of the Suburban as we jostled past empty campgrounds. "Don't take this the wrong way," I said, "but you don't look right as a civilian. I can't remember the last time I saw you without a gun at your hip and your badge clipped to your belt."

"Honey, I'll never be a civilian. I always have my badge and at least one gun on me at all times. Three-quarters of the state of Virginia is armed. I'd be crazy to go anywhere without one." He lifted the pant leg of his jeans so I could see the clutch piece he carried.

"Good point." Ever since I'd been attacked last winter I'd started carrying a gun—a black Beretta that fit my hand to perfection. I never left home without it. "When I was at the gun range last week Hilda Martin was in the lane next to me." The Martins owned the only grocery store in Bloody Mary. "She took out two of the overhead lights and shot the shit out of a concrete post before she emptied her magazine."

"Christ. Don't tell me that."

"Look on the bright side. If anyone robs the grocery store she'll probably scare them to death instead of leaving us with a body."

"Or take out six innocent bystanders."

"I told you to look on the bright side. You're on vacation. You need to lighten up."

Even with the high beams on it was hard to see the road in front of us. The park was thick with tall trees and they canopied over the road so there wasn't even a hint of moon-light. We passed picnic tables and a couple of cabins before the area opened up. Jones Pond sat dead in front of us, and the water was inky black and still. Police cars lined the road, their lights flashing a disorienting blue over the damp grass.

I parked the Suburban as close to the crime scene tape as I

could and turned off the motor. Jack and I got out and he took in the area with cop eyes while I went back to get my equipment.

Jack had done his time in the military after he'd graduated from college and then he'd gone on to be a SWAT cop in DC. He'd resigned after taking three bullets on a mission that had killed one of his closest friends, and then he'd come home to Bloody Mary to recover.

The sheriff's position had come open when the previous Sheriff had decided to retire abruptly and Jack had stepped into the role. He never talked about what had happened to him in DC, and I never pushed him to talk about it. I knew better than anyone that some personal demons were better left undisturbed.

The air coming in from the water was cold and smelled of brine and other things less pleasant. Jones Pond sat just on the edge of the shoreline, only a thin strip of land separating it from the Potomac River. Three large spotlights had been set up around the perimeter and lit the area well. The shoreline was muddy, so I pulled on my black coveralls and zipped them up to my chin. I slung my bag over my shoulder and ducked under the crime scene tape, Jack following close behind me.

"Doc Graves," Detective Colburn called out. "Thanks for coming. We're about done here, so he's all yours. Morning, Sheriff. You want in on this?"

"I'm on vacation."

"I'd heard a rumor." Colburn's lips twitched once and then went back into a thin line.

Colburn was about ten years older than me and Jack, making him in his early forties, and he had big city homicide experience, which was one of the reasons Jack had hired him. I don't know why Colburn had left the city for the small town way of life, but I'd noticed Jack had a lot of success recruiting cops that had more experience than a place like this warranted.

Colburn was tall, broad through the shoulders, and lean through the hips. His brown hair was graying at the temples, and he had cop's eyes of pale blue steel. A few months ago Colburn had been under investigation for the serial murders that had rocked our small community. He'd been having an affair with Amanda Wallace, the wife of one of the city councilmen, and her body had been discovered after she'd snuck away to meet with Colburn at a hotel.

Amanda had also been pregnant at the time of her death, so Colburn's world had been shaken off its axis in one fell swoop. He'd been cleared of murder, but I wasn't sure he'd ever get over losing the woman he loved and the child he hadn't known about.

Colburn mostly stayed to himself, and even if he had heard the gossip around town he probably wouldn't care much about it. But the people in this area had a long memory, and Colburn was still whispered about as a man who'd stolen another man's wife, and those same people held him responsible for her death, even though he hadn't been the one to tighten the noose around her neck. They'd never trust him again, and it had the potential to make things difficult farther down the road.

Colburn fell into step beside me as we made our way down to the body. "The 911 came in about three this morning. A couple of campers decided it would be fun to go skinny dipping in the middle of the night."

"Idiots," I said. "That water can't be more than forty degrees."

"Yeah, well, they're both twenty and had worked up their courage with a few beers. The girl sicked it all up as soon as she saw the body. They're sitting in the back of a squad car wrapped up in blankets. We'll talk to them again before we cut them loose, but I don't think there's much more we'll get from them."

The first thing I noticed about the body was his size. He was a big guy. Not overweight, but built more like Jack. A lot of muscles and bulk. He was dressed in a black T-shirt and matching cargo pants and his shoes and socks were missing.

"We found him just like this," Colburn said. "Face down in the mud. It was a hell of a mess when we turned him to get photos. I wanted you to get a feel for the scene so we put him back once we were through."

"I appreciate it," I said, kneeling next to the victim. I pulled gloves out of my bag and put them on and then handed Jack my recorder so I could keep my hands free. I touched my glove to the victim's skin and felt the give of the tissue.

"He's developed skin maceration, which tells me he's been in the water close to forty-eight hours. The skin has come loose and is peeling off in places. We'll have to be careful transporting him so we don't leave his outsides in the body bag. It's easier to know how long he's been in the water instead of time of death. The water messes with the stages of decomp. Lacerations on both arms and bottom of feet congruent with debris he ran into on his trip down the river. Did you find any ID on him?" I asked Colburn.

"No. No wallet and nothing in his pockets. No money either."

"Socks and shoes are gone."

"Yeah. Guy's settled down for an evening, kicking back and maybe watching some T.V."

"No rings on his fingers," I murmured, more to myself than anyone else. "But anything like that could have come off in the water. We'll have a hard time getting fingerprints. It'll be better to remove the skin from the fingers completely and try to get a solid print that way rather than transferring directly. It'll be too fragile."

I worked my way over the exposed skin to make sure I hadn't missed anything, but it was more than obvious what the cause of death was. I reached the back of the skull and was careful as I parted matted hair.

"Two gunshot wounds to the back of the head. Execution style. The holes are nice and neat." I retrieved a small ruler from the bag and measured the size of the holes and the distance between them.

Jack looked at the hole measurements and grunted. "Could be a couple of different handguns," he said. "It could be a .357 Magnum or a 9mm, but you'll have to send it off to ballistics to know for sure."

"Those were my thoughts as well," Colburn said. "And then I saw the front of him and now I'm leaning toward the .357 with hollow points. But like you said, ballistics will be able to tell us more."

"Let's turn him over," I said, more curious than ever about the front of the body.

Colburn already wore gloves, so he took the head and I took the feet and we carefully turned the victim over so he lay on his back.

"Damn. Martinez was right. He doesn't have a face," I said. I'd seen a lot of interesting things over the course of my tenure as an ER doctor and now as coroner, but I could honestly say the vacant face in front of me was something new.

The face was nothing more than spare bits of flesh and bone. The nose and mouth were empty holes, and the eye sockets were vacant—but I thought that might have more to do with the fish that had been snacking on the body for the last couple of days rather than the bullets themselves.

"High caliber weapon through the back of the head isn't going to leave much of anything when it comes out the other side," Jack said. "It's like dropping a pumpkin off the top of a building. I can see why you're thinking the .357 hollow points. Two shots to the back of the head will make anyone unrecognizable to their own mother."

Colburn grunted in agreement. "I've got Officer Chen looking for mob related crimes in the tri-state area because of the method of killing. A hit like this seems cold and calculated. No identification and he's dressed comfortably, so there's a possibility he was pulled from his house. Maybe something will click in the system."

"Who's Officer Chen?" I asked, not recognizing the name.

"She's only been on about a week," Jack said. "Good cop. She's the one talking to the kids who found the body."

I followed Jack's gaze toward the squad car and focused on the petite woman talking to the shaking kids. Her hair was glossy black and pulled back into a ponytail and her profile showed even features. She looked like a teenager instead of a cop.

"Don't let her fool you," Jack said, reading my mind. "Chen's got multiple black belts and put Martinez on his ass the first day on the job."

I snorted out a laugh at the mental picture. "I guess she wasn't impressed by the Martinez charm."

Jack smiled. "He's been keeping his distance ever since. Martinez doesn't meet a lot of women who don't fall all over themselves to get his attention, but Chen looked at him like he was selling vacuum cleaners door to door and turned her back."

"It'll do him some good," Colburn said. "A little humility never hurt anyone."

"Where did Chen come from?" I asked.

"She worked the streets in Atlanta. Mostly inner city. It was her home turf and she was comfortable there."

"King George County is a long way from inner city Atlanta. How's she liking the slow life?"

I felt Jack's shrug beside me. "She was one of the responding officers on the Greenwood Elementary shooting."

"Jesus," I whispered. "I can't imagine."

The Greenwood Elementary Shooting had been national news for weeks now. Five high schoolers had made a suicide pact and decided along the way they were going to take as many members of their small town that they could with them. They'd started with the elementary school. That's where it had ended too. Sixty-two children and teachers dead.

"Yeah. Chen did the work and waded through the blood, and then when it was all over she went to her chief and turned in her badge and gun. Chief Walker and I are friends, so he gave me a call and told me she was too good a cop to not work the job at all. That maybe she just needed a change of pace. It didn't take much to convince her to pick up a badge again. Cop to the bone. Sometimes you just need a little break."

I ducked my head so Jack wouldn't see my smile. All his cops were cops to the bone, but they all had stories and pasts that haunted them. The sheriff's office was turning into a kind of rehabilitation center, and I wondered if Jack realized what he was doing. I snuck a glance at him from the corner of my eye and saw he was watching me. Of course he knew what he was doing. Nothing much got past Jack.

I turned my attention back to the body and then looked at Colburn. "I didn't realize we were in mob territory. We're a long way from Jersey and Vegas."

"But we're a stone's throw from Washington D.C., and the mob and politics have gone hand in hand since the dawn of time. If the vic's from that area it could be politically motivated. Or it could be none of the above."

"I'll see if I can find any wounds ante mortem. Maybe he put up a fight. But like I said, at this point it'll be hard to determine what was caused by fighting and what was caused by the river."

Colburn squatted down next to the body but across from me. "We've had a lot of rain the last couple of days. The river is moving more than usual. This guy could be from any state that butts up against the Potomac River. I've got Lewis checking missing persons just to make sure. If you think he's been dead at least forty-eight hours then a report should've been filed by now. If we can get an ID on him soon we'll be able to determine if he's one of ours. If he's not we'll have to give him over to another jurisdiction."

I looked back at the body and stuck my finger into the mouth cavity. "The bullet fractured teeth. It'll make it harder to get a dental match. And the condition of the skin after sitting in water all this time is going to make retrieving the fingerprints difficult. I'll work on the identification and then keep him on ice until we know for sure if he's ours."

"Anything wash up with him?" Jack asked.

Colburn looked up and down the shoreline to where the circle from the spotlights ended. "Not that we've found so far. When daylight hits we'll comb as far as we can and see what's what."

"All right. Let's bag him up and get him to the lab. It'll take a little time to get the prints. It's delicate work. But I should be able to have them to you in a few hours. Maybe sooner now that I have an assistant."

I looked over at Jack and grinned. Everyone knew Jack was a hell of a cop and there wasn't much that bothered him. The autopsies didn't faze him one bit. But I only had one lab, and when I needed to put on my coroner cap I had to do autopsies in the same place where I prepared bodies for burial, and the smell of embalming fluid was enough to send Jack over the edge every time. It was an acquired smell—one I'd been used to since childhood.

The great thing about Jack was that he was also a perverse creature by nature, and just the fact that I'd thrown down the gauntlet would mean he'd feel obligated to accept my challenge in becoming my assistant for the day. I knew Jack as well as he knew me.

His face was a tad green, but his smile was sharp and a little bit cocky. "At your service, Doctor Graves."

3

DAWN WAS JUST PEEKING OVER THE HORIZON BY THE TIME WE drove back into Bloody Mary, Jack behind the wheel this time.

I'd done a lot of thinking over the past half-hour in the car, and I knew I was the one who needed to make the change. These were my hang-ups. And Jack was right; it was my fear holding us back.

I'd watched a man I'd been intimate with die in front of me. I hadn't loved him—not the way I'd wanted to—but there'd still been something there. Something inside of me had broken that day, but I knew it would be nothing in comparison if anything ever happened to Jack. I wouldn't just be broken. I'd be shattered.

The paths we'd chosen kept death in the forefront of our lives —a constant reminder that the time we had on earth was finite—and that the human body was fragile. I could either live with that fear and that reminder swallowing me whole on a daily basis, or I could live the life I'd been given a second chance at with Jack at my side.

"If we got married," I said softly, my gaze turned toward the window so the buildings went by in a blur. "I think I'd want to take your name. If you don't mind." My face was hot with embarrassment and I wondered why I'd even brought it up. Hadn't even known I'd been thinking about it somewhere in my subconscious.

"Oh, yeah?" Jack answered casually, but I knew I had his full attention.

"It's just that I was thinking the name Graves is not really mine to begin with. They weren't my parents. We don't—"

My throat was dry and I would've given anything for a glass of water. My voice would never be the same after my incident. The doctors had told me that. And they'd said there would be some days worse than others, when the words wouldn't come at all. I cleared my throat and tried again.

"We don't share blood. So it's not like I'm really holding onto anything of value."

He reached across and took my hand, squeezing it lightly. "You know I'd be honored for you to take my name. But I want you to do it because it's what you really want. Not because it's what you think you should do. And not as a shield to hide whom you are. You're not of their blood, and I'm damned happy about that if you want to know the truth. But you've made your name what it is, Jaye. Not them. They had nothing to do with it. Just remember that when you're signing on the dotted line."

"My first name is stupid," I blurted out. I figured if I was going to embarrass myself I should go ahead and get it all out of the way. "I just wanted you to know that because you'll probably see it on an official document. If we get married, I mean."

"I'm glad that you can talk about getting married to me now without looking like you're going to throw up. We're making progress. And I'm assuming all this talk of marriage means that you're in agreement to doing it sooner rather than later?"

I chewed at my bottom lip and realized how stiff I was when my shoulders started to hurt. I took a deep breath and relaxed. I loved Jack. I knew that would never change. It was time for me to make a decision and commit instead of worrying about what might happen. And it was time I stopped letting the actions of my parents dictate the rest of my life. I'd tell Jack about my father, we'd deal with the body and the papers, and then we'd get married. As long as he was in my life I could deal with anything else.

"Yeah." I finally turned in my seat until I was facing him. We came to a stoplight and he looked at me—his eyes filled with a little bit of laughter and a lifetime of love. "I'm ready whenever you are."

His sensual lips curved upward and I felt the slow burn of arousal roll through my body. I wondered if it would ever get old—looking at the sheer maleness of him and feeling my bones turn liquid and my heart flip in my chest.

"And just so there are no surprises," he said. "I've known your real name since we were in fifth grade. I've been holding back the information for a potential blackmail opportunity."

My mouth dropped open in surprise and I felt the flush of

embarrassment creep up my neck and cheeks. "All this time and you never said anything?"

"I've thought about it many times over the years. I came really close to using it once or twice, but I could never get it to come out. The name doesn't fit you."

I sunk down in the seat a bit and crossed my arms over my chest. "Well thank God for that. What kind of respectable doctor is named Jericho? And what the hell were my parents thinking? It's like they stole me just so they could make my life miserable. What kind of people do that?"

"The shitty kind, apparently. Don't worry, love. Your secret is safe with me."

———

GRAVES FUNERAL HOME sat right on the corner of Anne Boleyn and Catherine of Aragon, and it took up two full lots. It was a three-story Colonial with dark red brick and white columns that flanked the front entryway. Two massive elm trees stood in front of the house, the leaves new with spring and bright green. No grass grew beneath the trees, and the roots were gnarled and grew out of the ground, cracking the sidewalk.

Jack backed the Suburban up under the portico where we loaded and unloaded bodies. It didn't take long to get the victim moved onto a stretcher and up the ramp that led into the large kitchen. This was the private area of the funeral home where guests weren't allowed. The big stainless steel door that led to my lab was just off the kitchen, and I keyed in the code and waited until the locks released.

Frigid air blasted me in the face as soon as I opened the door and Jack and I maneuvered the body inside and to the elevator. Despite the temperature, sweat broke out on Jack's brow as soon as the smell of the embalming fluid hit him. I immediately went and turned on the fans to the highest setting.

I tried not to pay any attention to the five boxes that sat unobtrusively in the corner—the same boxes my father had been looking for. This was the only secure place I could keep them, but I wondered if the security on the door would really keep him out. Jack had a large safe in his closet where he kept extra guns, a few heirlooms, and extra cash. I was thinking it might be better to move them there, that way we could go through the boxes in the comfort of our home instead of huddled in the basement with a dead body.

"You okay?" I asked after I got the body settled on the table. "There are bottles of water in the fridge if you want one."

"I'm good. It'll pass after a few minutes."

I grabbed a fresh pair of gloves and then tossed him the box. I worried about the shape the victim would be in even after such a short trip in the car. Victims found in the water after an extended period of time were extremely delicate, and I knew if I was going to get viable prints for Colburn the work was going to be painstakingly tedious.

I unzipped the body bag and we carefully removed the victim, making sure not to brush against his sensitive skin. I cut his shirt down the middle and peeled it away from his chest and shoulders. His flesh was already patchy and raw in places just from the trip down the river. My complete attention was on getting the sleeve from the arm when I felt Jack pause.

I looked up to make sure he was all right and wasn't going to be sick, but I knew it was something else entirely once I saw the look on his face.

"What's wrong?"

"Look at the tattoo on his chest."

Just above the victim's heart was a tattoo of an eagle. It held an assault rifle in one talon, a lightning bolt in the other, and a large knife pierced the center. The detail was incredible and I could recite everything about it without looking at it. I was intimately familiar with that tattoo. Jack had one just like it, only his was located above his right hip.

"I don't understand."

"He was a SWAT brother," Jack said. "Or maybe a wannabe, but he's got marks of combat on him—looks like a knife wound on the arm and a bullet hole down low on his side—so I'm thinking he's probably legit. We all have the tattoo. It's a rite of passage."

"One of your squad from DC? Is the tattoo specific to which unit you're in or are they all the same?"

"They're all the same, so he could be from anywhere. But since he washed up on our shore, he's more than likely out of one of the surrounding offices. If he's a cop his prints will be easy to tag."

"Then I'll get started. This is going to take a while if you've got something else you want to do."

"I'll see it through."

I finished removing the victim's clothes and bagged them carefully to send off to Richmond and the lab techs we used there. Just in case there was blood belonging to someone other than the victim.

The tissue on the victim's fingers wasn't stable, and if I wasn't careful I'd tear the skin and wouldn't get a viable print. The easiest way to do it was to remove the finger entirely and then remove the skin. It was quick—if gruesome —work to remove the finger and the skin, and I laid the epidermis on the table.

I used a superglue solution to spray on the skin to keep it from tearing and then I carefully wrapped it over my glove, on the tip of my index finger. The black powder used at crime scenes was more delicate than the ink normally used when fingerprinted at the station, so Jack dusted the finger and I gently pressed it to the card he'd placed on the table. It was slow work, but when I lifted my hand and saw the perfect print I knew we'd gotten what we needed.

I wiped my brow with the back of my arm, and when I stood up straight my back ached from where I'd been hunched over. I looked at the clock and saw we'd been at it for almost three hours. It was shy of noon and my stomach rumbled, reminding me I'd had nothing more than a cup of coffee all day.

"That's all I can do for now until I get the go ahead to start on an autopsy."

"Then let's get this to Colburn so he can look for matches through the computer. If the victim's a cop he'll be much easier to find. And while we're out we can grab some lunch at Martha's."

Martha's Diner was the only sit down restaurant in Bloody Mary. The hamburgers were good and greasy, the coffee questionable, and the pie out of this world. "Oh, good. It's been a couple of days since I've been stared at and gossiped about. I was starting to miss it."

"I'm sensing sarcasm in your tone."

I stuck out my tongue at Jack and pushed the body into the walk-in freezer. "You're asking for it. You know Martha is going to ask you all sorts of questions about our relationship, and then you'll tell her we're engaged. And then she's going to want to know why I'm not wearing an engagement ring. Then she's going to assume it's because you're still on the market and she'll try to fix you up with her niece's grand-daughter's first cousin."

"I'm pretty sure I followed your entire train of thought," Jack said wryly. "It must be love."

I stripped off my gloves, tossing them in the trash, and rolled my eyes.

"Besides," he said. "I have your engagement ring in the safe. If you'd like we can get it from the house before we go eat lunch so we can avoid Martha's prying."

Jack was already halfway up the stairs, while I stood with my mouth open at the thought of a ring. A ring made it real. Not to mention I was terrified of losing it. I'd never worn jewelry before. It had a tendency to end up in whatever body I had cut open on my table.

"What—You already have a ring? How? Why?"

He paused on the stairs and looked back at me. "You're full of questions today. The ring belonged to my great-grand-mother and it's a family tradition to pass it down to the oldest son's bride. But if you don't like it we'll find something else."

"No! Of course I'll like it. I'm just—surprised. I hadn't actually thought that far ahead."

The look he gave me wasn't discernable, and he turned back toward the top of the stairs. I started up after him and had my foot on the first step when the boxes caught my eye. What the hell, I thought. It was a day for changes.

"Jack." He stopped at the top, his hand on the door, and looked back down at me. "I think I want to move the boxes home." I realized it was the first time I'd referred to his house as my home. It was still a new experience for me to think of sharing my life with someone. With sharing a house. "I was thinking I should start going through them tonight."

"You don't have to do it alone."

"I was hoping you'd say that." And while we were going through the boxes—examining the secrets my parents kept—I'd tell him my father wasn't really dead. And then we'd see what happened.

Jack nodded and started back down the stairs to lift the boxes. They weren't overly heavy—about a foot deep and wide—and we were able to carry two each up the stairs and load them into the back of the Suburban. I got in the passenger seat while Jack retrieved the remaining box.

The drive to the police station didn't take long. All of the municipal buildings were built in the county square, so law and order was equal in all four of the towns that made up King George County—Bloody Mary and King George proper to the north and Nottingham and Newcastle to the south.

The courthouse sat in the center of the county square—Gothic and intimidating—three full stories of carved stone and hallowed hallways of generations past. The goddesses of justice and mercy loomed at each corner, but unless you knew who they were supposed to be there was no way to recognize them, considering the sculptor must have been drunk and had a fetish for hunchbacked gargoyle-looking women.

The police station sat to the left of the courthouse, much more sedate in appearance—a pale bricked building shaped like a rectangle that hadn't been updated since 1973. The fire station sat to the right, looking much like every other fire station in the state of Virginia.

Jack parked in his assigned spot in front of the station but left the motor running so I could run the fingerprints inside to Colburn.

"I'm not sure you should be using this space—which is clearly reserved for a servant of the city—while you're on vacation." I batted my eyelashes at Jack playfully and opened the car door. "There has to be some kind of ordinance against it."

"If not, it's probably your civic duty to propose one at the next city council meeting." Jack's gaze was amused.

King George County had a reputation of passing ordinances that made absolutely no sense whatsoever—like not allowing pets to be the sole heir to a fortune or not allowing people inside the city limits to water their lawns after five o'clock on a Thursday.

"You never know. In the next couple of months, this parking spot might belong to someone else."

"It's a good thing I'm marrying you for your money then." I brought my legs back inside the car and closed the door. "Is it bothering you?" I asked. "The possibility of losing the election?"

"No. Not really. I'm more worried about winning the election."

I watched him carefully for a couple of minutes, but he stared straight ahead, his fingers tapping on the steering wheel. And then it hit me like a bolt of lightning. "You don't want to be Sheriff."

He shrugged. "I like being a cop. And being Sheriff here served its purpose after I left the city and came back to recover. But the politics in this town pisses me off and it feels like I'm settling more disputes among the city council and the mayor's office than doing any real police work. Especially since the investigation started on the Aryan Nation. It's been a clusterfuck considering half the damn people sitting in seats of some importance have been removed or arrested."

Only a couple of weeks before we'd uncovered a decades long secret in our small town of hate and prejudice, and it took the death of one of the ministers at the Presbyterian church for it to all be uncovered.

"I'd be lying if I said I hadn't been seriously considering a few of the offers that have come my way."

I didn't know what to say. I was speechless. And embarrassed that I hadn't noticed his dissatisfaction before. "God, Jack. Why didn't you say something sooner?"

"I don't really have anything to complain about. And I'm not really dissatisfied. This is familiar and I have good men and women under my command. Sometimes I just miss the thrill. The adrenaline rush. It wasn't an easy change going from SWAT in a city like DC, where business is booming and you're living for that adrenaline high that each op brings. There's nothing like it. But coming here—it was like doing ninety miles an hour and then slamming on the brakes. I guess I needed it at the time—mentally as well as physically —but it's started to bother me more than usual lately."

"I'm sorry." I put my hand on his and squeezed gently. "You know I'm okay with whatever you want to do. If you want to make a change."

He smiled and squeezed my hand back. "I'm not going to think about it too much for the next six weeks. Maybe I just need a break and I'll feel differently once I come back. Or maybe I really am worried about the election. I've pissed off a lot of people since I've been sheriff."

"Most of them are the single women who are going to be heartbroken you're no longer available."

"You mean I have to stop dating now that we're together?" he asked, the outraged shock clear on his face.

I snorted out a laugh and opened the car door again. "You'd better. Or Colburn will be investigating your murder next. Though it shouldn't be too hard to figure out how you died with all my embalming equipment hooked up to your twitching body."

"Harsh, Doctor Graves. And inventive. Your intelligence and creativity continue to turn me on."

"Jesus. You're sick."

"Maybe you can cure me later."

4

"IT'S GOING TO RAIN AGAIN," JACK SAID AS WE PARKED IN front of Martha's Diner. "At least before dark."

"It must be your farming skills that make you predict the weather with such accuracy." Jack came from a long line of tobacco farmers, but for the past two generations the Lawson men hadn't spent a lot of time out in the fields working the land. They mostly just enjoyed investing their money and pursuing the things that interested them.

Jack grinned and we got out of the Suburban and headed inside. Grilled onions and grease assaulted us as soon as we walked through the doors and conversation came to a stand still. It was right in the middle of the lunch rush, so the silence made quite an impact.

Jack and I made our way to one of the turquoise Formica tables and the voices whooshed into conversation again. The vinyl seats were cracked with age and I let Jack have the side that faced the entryway. He hated sitting with his back to a door.

"Well, look what the cat dragged in." Martha Smith swung out of the kitchen with half a dozen plates stacked on her arms and managed to make it look graceful as she dropped off food from table to table.

She'd been serving burgers and giving hell to her customers for sixty years. I had no idea how old she was, but her hair was dyed fire engine red and the lines on her face were deep and numerous. Her lipstick matched her hair and her dingy white apron wrapped twice around her tiny frame.

"Long time no see, Sheriff. Doc Graves." She nodded to us both and whipped out the ragged pad she kept in her apron pocket. "Though can't say I blame ya. I've heard nothing for the past two weeks but how the two of you were shacked up together living in sin. That's the best way if you ask me."

She pursed her lips and arched a penciled brow. "I always thought sin was way more fun than marriage. Husbands are a pain in the ass. I should know since I've had four of them. And then I managed to birth eight boys who aren't any better at marriage than their fathers were. Though I'm not sure Jimmy belonged to any of my husbands. He never has been right in the head and he was conceived about the time that traveling revival came through town."

I kept my head buried in one of the plastic menus that sat behind the miniature jukeboxes on the table.

"You think I'm going to be a pain in the ass, Jaye?" Jack asked. I could hear the smile in his voice.

"More than likely. You've been doing a pretty good job of it for the last thirty years. You might as well continue the streak for the next fifty or so."

Marta cackled and slapped her notepad on her thigh. "Well I'll be. Does that mean congratulations are in order? I sure as hell hope so. I've got fifty bucks riding on the two of you."

"We're still in the planning stages," Jack said tactfully. "But we plan to get married soon."

"How come I don't see a ring? It's not legitimate until there's a ring on your finger, girl. I thought you knew better than that."

I looked up long enough to narrow my eyes at Jack and glare, but he just winked back at me. "We'll take two burgers made how we like them and the fries crispy. Iced tea to drink."

"Humph," Martha said. "You can't keep it a secret for long. Good thing your mama is coming in to pick up an order soon. I'll get all the details from her."

Jack and I looked at each other and froze, my eyes widening in panic. Jack didn't ruffle easy, and if I didn't know him so well I wouldn't have been able to see the *Oh, shit* look on his face beneath the placid façade.

Martha *hmphed* again and went off to the kitchen.

"I take it you haven't mentioned marriage to your mother," I asked stiffly. My feelings were hurt, though I wasn't completely sure why considering I hadn't been all that much in favor of it to begin with.

"Actually, I have," he said. "Several months ago, as a matter of fact."

"I'm sorry? What?" I shook my head hoping it would clear the cobwebs and things would start to make sense. "We weren't even together months ago."

"I remember," he said, lips twitching. "You were hurt and hiding. It didn't seem like the time to bring it up. But my mother knows me well and knew I was about at the end of my rope as far as waiting for you. She'll be thrilled. I'd just hoped to tell her without dozens of ears listening in on the conversation."

Martha brought back our drinks and burgers in no time and we settled in to eat. About that time the front door opened again and Jack's mother walked inside. Mrs. Lawson was a tiny woman—maybe an inch over five feet—and it never ceased to amaze me that she'd managed to produce a son the size of Jack. Her hair was as dark as her son's, but her eyes were a blue so pale it was almost startling. Her skin was smooth and the lines around her eyes hinted at good humor and a lot of laughter.

Jack got up from the booth and intercepted her in a big bear hug before she could reach the counter and the bags of food waiting there for her. He plucked her right off the ground and squeezed her tight. I couldn't hear what he said but whatever it was made her laugh.

"Put me down you fool, and let me say hi to J.J." Mrs. Lawson swatted him on the shoulder and he sat her gently on her feet. "How's my girl doing?" she asked, bending down to wrap me in her arms.

The endearment made me smile. I'd been *her girl* for as long as I could remember. She'd always been the one I'd gone to when my feelings had been hurt or I had scrapes or bruises to get cleaned up—which was often considering I hung out with a pack of boys most of my childhood. It had been her shoulder I cried on after my first broken heart and she'd been the one to walk me through the embarrassment of my first period. My own mother had always been too busy with work, which I knew now consisted of smuggling items hidden in the bodies that moved in and out of the funeral home.

"I'm doing good," I said, squeezing her back, maybe a little harder and more desperate than I meant to. She leaned back and took my face between her hands and studied me long and hard, and then she nodded in what I assumed was satisfaction.

"When are you going to make an honest man out of my son?" She scooted into the booth next to me and gave me an impish smile.

"Apparently soon if your son has anything to say about it."

"I can't tell you how nervous it makes me for you both to be staring at me like that," Jack said.

"Good," she nodded. "Make sure you get your Great-Grandmother Lawson's ring. People will start to talk if she doesn't have a ring on her finger."

"I'm on it," Jack said. "How come you never wore the Lawson ring? I'd never really thought much about it until I pulled it out the other day to look at."

"I told you your father and I eloped." She turned to look at me with a sparkle in her eyes and a mischievous tilt to her mouth. "A group of us ended up in Las Vegas for a weekend, and Rich and I certainly knew each other but we weren't exactly in a romantic relationship if you know what I mean."

Jack groaned and I couldn't help but smile at his discomfort.

"Needless to say, there was something about Sin City that changed things between the two of us," she went on. "We found ourselves married by the time the trip was over. Rich bought me this ring at the chapel where we married." She held out her hand and I looked at the gold band with barely a chip of a diamond in the center.

"He was barely twenty-one at the time and hadn't come into his trust fund yet, so it was what he could afford. By the time we got back home and explained everything to our parents, I'd gotten attached to it and didn't want to wear the Lawson ring. Not to mention your father would've had to pry that ring off your grandmother's cold dead hand before she gave it to me willingly. I always thought that ring was too good for her anyway. Good thing she died before you came along, J.J."

"Wow, Mom. Why don't you tell us how you really feel?" Jack said.

Mrs. Lawson smiled at her son and stole a fry off his plate.

"So she wouldn't have liked me?" I asked, wondering how big of an impact marriage would make on his respectable family—a family that came from old money and traditions.

"That woman didn't like anyone. A very disagreeable person in general, but she had a ton of money and the marriage made good sense businesswise. You're just what we need in this family to shake things up a bit." She waggled her eyebrows comically. "Jack's uncles and cousins are a little staid. Meaning they're boring as hell. We try not to see them very often. That's why we travel so much over the holidays."

"A good tradition for us to start too," Jack agreed.

Mrs. Lawson scooted out of the booth. "I've got to get back to the house with the food before your father sends a search party after me. Congratulations to you both." She bent down and hugged Jack tightly. "It's about damned time if you ask me." She leaned down to hug me again too and whispered in my ear, "I always thought of you as a daughter. It'll be nice to make it permanent."

Tears stung my eyes as she left money on the counter and grabbed her food. "She's a good mom," I said.

"The best."

We finished up our food in silence and Jack left a generous tip with the bill. We snuck out while Martha was busy in the kitchen so we couldn't get waylaid again.

"So how do you feel about eloping?" Jack asked when we got back in the Suburban.

"If it means there's no one there but you and me and we get to have sex afterwards then I'm all for it."

"I can almost guarantee there will be sex afterward. Probably several times." He pulled out of the parking lot and headed in the opposite direction on Queen Mary, away from the funeral home and the rest of town. It took us higher in elevation, the trees becoming denser and the houses fewer and farther between. Only one road intersected with Queen Mary on this side of town—Heresy Road.

If we'd turned left it would've taken us back to the house I'd grown up in—the house where I'd seen the ghost of my father the day before. It seemed like a lifetime ago. But instead of turning left toward my past, Jack turned right. Toward my future.

Jack's house—our house—jutted up from the cliff majestically, as if it were part of the landscape itself. It was a log cabin of two stories, but not like any cabin I'd seen before. The logs were smoothed to an amber gleam and grey stone chimneys rose from each end of the house. A wide porch wrapped around all sides. There weren't many windows in the front, but the back of the house was nothing but windows that looked out over towering trees so thick you couldn't see the river below. It was more space than we needed. Even if we someday filled it with children it would be too much.

Most people underestimated Jack. They saw him as the son of wealthy tobacco farmers, a little reckless and with a temper that had plagued him when he was younger. They saw him as someone who craved the wild side of life, fast cars and fast women, but with a sharp and complex brain that made him a great cop. He had Master's Degrees in both criminal justice and psychology.

But what they didn't know about Jack was that he loved his solitude—his quiet spot on the side of a cliff that was completely private and closed off from the outside world. He liked good wine and intelligent conversation. And when he needed to think something through, he more likely than not did it in the kitchen cooking something that would make the mouth salivate and tastebuds explode.

I'd been thinking about the body that had washed up on shore. It was puzzling, and I'd be lying if I said I wasn't curious to know more about it.

"I keep thinking about the victim," I said. "There was nothing familiar about him? Other than the tattoo, I mean?"

Jack was busy removing the boxes from the back of the Suburban and I joined in to help.

"It's not like I could ID him from his face. It's been six years since I was SWAT. I've stayed in touch with my brothers over the years, but we all have our own lives, our own families.

Some transferred to other cities. A couple have passed away over the last few months. The rest are scattered here and there. Only a couple stayed with the team."

"It was that bad?" I asked, referring to the last op that had left Jack fighting for his life.

He looked at me out of somber eyes, his face blank of emotion. It was the same face he used whenever we were at a crime scene. A face that didn't want anyone to know what he was thinking or feeling.

"Yeah, it was that bad."

5

THE BOXES SAT IN A NEAT ROW ON THE DINING ROOM TABLE. When I'd found them in the bunker, along with the dead body, I'd taken them almost out of reflex. I'd made the mistake of opening one of the boxes, kneeling on the concrete floor of the bunker next to the dead man. Inside it had been my birth records—my *original* birth records. Not the ones my parents had forged to pass me off as their own. I knew my real parents' names and where they came from. The circumstances of their death.

I'd read through each scrap until I was numb with cold and anger. And then I'd sealed all the boxes tightly with packing tape, transferred them to my car, and driven away without looking back. I couldn't imagine what else could be worse than discovering the parents that had raised you weren't your own, but if it were possible, the worse would be in the other boxes.

Jack made a fresh pot of coffee and I opened the pocketknife with fumbling fingers, wondering where to start first.

"I guess there's no time like the present," I whispered.

Jack sat our coffee on the table and took my wrist before I could cut into the first box, and I gave him a questioning look.

"If the FBI finds out about these boxes, they'll be all over you and the contents before you can blink. It'll make you an accessory after the fact. And it could cast suspicion again on your involvement prior to their death."

I licked my lips but my mouth was dry as dust at Jack's words. "I know that. I know this is hard for you. Straddling the line between following and breaking the law."

He blew out a breath in exasperation and gave my wrist a squeeze. "Dammit, Jaye. It doesn't matter what I think or feel. I stand with you. Always. And the point I was trying to make was that I wouldn't blame you if you set fire to the whole lot of it. Maybe there are things in there you're better off not knowing. Maybe things that don't ever need to be brought into the light of day. It could cause more questions than there are to answer."

I leaned in and kissed Jack softly. "Thank you for saying that. But you know as well as I do we need to do this. Just like I know if there's something in here that the FBI needs to know that you'll pass it along to them. Your integrity is part of who you are. And I wouldn't ask you to change or compromise that integrity for me."

I stepped up to the first box and sliced it neatly down the center seam. I folded the flaps open and sat the knife down on the table. Probably a good idea considering how badly my hands were shaking.

I recognized the neatly labeled files right away. My name was printed in block lettering on the one on top and the ink was smeared slightly where my tears had fallen.

"This is the one I opened already. It's got all of my birth records, as well as the hospital records on my mother when she was shot and lost her own baby. It also gives detailed records of what they smuggled back in the bodies of my real parents and the other military personnel they transported back to the US."

Jack stayed silent but I caught the muscles of his jaw clench out of my periphery. He took out the individual files and flipped through them briefly. I didn't need to see the contents again so I moved on to the next box.

They were getting easier to open. My lungs weren't quite as tight as they'd been when we'd first started. I sliced the second box and pulled back the flaps and then gasped at the contents.

"Holy shit," I croaked out.

Jack looked up sharply and grabbed my hands before I could reach into the box. "Hold on a second. Let's put on gloves. It'll make things less complicated later."

Stacks of crisp hundred dollar bills were banded together and lined up neatly. The money looked new and each group still had the bank wrapper around it so it was divided into ten thousand dollar stacks.

Jack handed me a pair of spare gloves and I snapped them on. "I guess this was their version of a savings account. I've heard of people putting their money in a shoebox under the bed, but never in a bunker with a corpse."

"Banks have shitty interest at the moment. Maybe the corpse offered them a better deal."

"Jesus, Jack," I said, rolling my eyes.

He pulled the money out and set it on the table. "An even two million dollars." He pulled one of the bills out and held it up to the light. "And it's real as far as I can tell, or the best counterfeit I've ever come across. A nice nest egg in case of an emergency. How many accounts did the FBI seize when they started the investigation into your parents?"

"There were the regular accounts at the local bank, both personal and business. They had a couple of savings accounts as well, a retirement account, and a brokerage account. All of the money in them was normal for people of their age, careers, and income. Then they had the four offshore accounts, each under different aliases. The smallest was just over a million dollars. The largest had just under sixteen million. The FBI wasn't really forthcoming with information after that. I don't know if they ever found out where the money came from. If they did, they didn't share that news with me."

"So another two million in cash just to be safe. Your parents were planners. They'd have an escape if things started to go to shit—money, IDs, safehouses."

I stared down at the money, knowing if Jack could see my face he'd be able to tell what I was thinking. My parents *had* had a contingency plan in place. They'd faked their death by driving their car over a cliff and staged it to look like a lovers' quarrel turned suicide. They'd planted the scenes nicely. Arguing loudly at the restaurant where they'd had dinner over a man who'd shown too much attention to my mother—a man she'd supposedly acted too familiar with.

There'd been other fights and a shoving match that had garnered attention from the local police. They'd had too much to drink and had gotten in the little two-seater convertible my dad had rebuilt, and then they'd sped down the narrow two-lane road up the side of the mountain, swerving to avoid cars head on.

There had been witnesses that had seen them drive over the side of the mountain. They saw the car swerve out of control and they all said there'd been no sign that the brakes had been used. The cops were quick to label it a double suicide after the way my parents had set the stage. They didn't investigate much at all. And the bodies they'd recovered from the scene had been beyond recognition. Only dental records had confirmed their deaths, and obviously that had been as big a lie as the rest of it.

"I'll start on the next one while you deal with that," I said. I sliced into the third box and wasn't surprised to see passports, cell phones, and driver's licenses under multiple names. "Guess you were right about the planning."

I was almost on autopilot now, slicing and dumping the contents, scanning through them quickly while my heart raced inside my chest. This what my father had come back for. Money and fake IDs so he could slip through the cracks. He hadn't come back for me. To tell me it had all been a big misunderstanding. That I had the wrong idea about the kind of people he and my mother had been.

Jack's hand squeezed my shoulder and I dropped my head down, bracing my hands against the table.

"It doesn't get any easier," I said. "Every time I think I've put it behind me I see the proof of what they were. For a long time after the FBI came to question me I lived in a state of denial, even though they had irrefutable proof. I couldn't believe that all of that had happened right under my nose. That my own parents had lied to me and betrayed me."

"It shouldn't make you feel guilty that you love them. They're your parents, Jaye. You want them to be good and honest and kind. And it doesn't make you less that you still have hope for that somewhere inside you. Their job was to love and protect you. It's not your shame but theirs that they couldn't manage to do it."

As usual Jack cut right to the heart of the matter. Despite it all, I did still love them. They were my parents, and blood was supposed to be thicker than water. But there was no blood either. Just lies.

"Sometimes that psychology degree comes in handy," I said, trying to lighten the mood.

He kissed the back of my neck softly. "I love you. Just remember that."

"I do. Every day. And I'm amazed by it. Humbled by it."

I cleared my throat and moved to the next box. My hand was steadier as I sliced through the tape. The box rattled as I moved it and piqued my curiosity.

"Flash drives. What do you want to bet we're not going to like whatever we find on them?" The box was filled with silver flash drives, neatly labeled with a series of numbers, almost like binary coding found in a library.

"If your parents were as careful as I think they were, they'll all be encrypted. I've got some skills in that area, but I'd be slow and I wouldn't want to trigger any deletions if I made a mistake. Carver would be able to help us if I asked. He's a freaking genius with computers."

Ben Carver was a close friend of Jack's and one of the few FBI agents who could be in the same vicinity as me without questioning me for illegal activity. He'd helped us on cases before and he was a good guy. But I didn't know if I'd be comfortable, even with someone like Ben, knowing what might be on those flash drives.

"I'll think about it."

There was one box left and I grabbed for the coffee cup Jack had sat on the table. I took a sip and realized it had gone cold. I went to the sink and poured it out and then got myself a fresh cup.

"I need to tell you something." I turned back to face Jack. What I had to say deserved to be said face to face.

His brows raised. "Do I need to sit down for this?"

"It probably wouldn't hurt."

He pulled out one of the dining chairs and took a seat, leaning his arms on the table. "Are you finally going to tell me what's been bothering you?"

Quick. Like a Band-Aid, I thought.

"I saw my father yesterday."

"I beg your pardon?" He looked more concerned than alarmed, and I wondered if he thought I was having some sort of psychotic episode.

"I'm serious. He was there when I walked into the house yesterday. Just walked right out of the dark like a fucking ghost. But he was real enough." I took the silver ring he'd given me out of my pocket and tossed it on the table, and we both watched it bounce a couple of times before it spun to a stop.

"My mother's wedding ring. She would have been wearing it when they went over the side of the mountain. But obviously it wasn't them in the car. He's alive. And he's here in Bloody Mary."

Jack was silent for a long while. He picked the ring up and held it between his thumb and forefinger and then stared at me out of hurt and angry eyes. "What the fuck, Jaye? Why didn't you tell me?"

I knew the signs of Jack's temper. He'd gotten a hold of it since his misspent youth, and he had a much longer fuse now, so it was slower to burn.

"I'm telling you now." My own temper was frayed at the edges, and the night's lack of sleep caused a vicious headache to pound behind my eyes. "I just had to get a handle on it."

"By yourself. Because God forbid you lean on anyone or take any help from anyone. And while you were getting a handle on it a known felon and possible murderer is walking the streets."

"He took me by surprise. And he's my father."

"And I'm the goddamned Sheriff. I had a right to know. And it doesn't matter that he's your father. I have a duty to bring him in. The law is the law."

"Easy how quickly you become the sheriff instead of my partner," I said, going cold inside. "And I'm not trying to break the law. I just needed a few fucking hours to wrap my head around the fact that the man I buried two years ago is alive and well. So fuck you and the law. Really, I appreciate you taking the time to ask how well I'm dealing with all this instead of jumping straight into telling me you're going to hunt him down and arrest him."

My face was hot with anger and my hands shook. Short breaths made my lungs heave and I wanted nothing more than to throw the coffee cup across the room and watch it smash into a million pieces.

"Jaye—" he growled and rubbed his hands through his hair like he always did when he was agitated. "Fine. You've had your few hours to get used to it. I'll even put the law aside for the moment. But you should have trusted me enough to tell me the minute I drove up to the house."

"Why, so you could pull your high and mighty sheriff routine?"

"Don't push me right now. I need you to fill me in on the details so we can start a search in the area." He grabbed a notepad and pen from his bag, and the notepad slapped against the table where he dropped it. "It looks like I won't be taking that vacation after all."

I jerked back against the counter and my shoulders stiffened with pride. I guessed if he wasn't taking a vacation then that meant that we weren't getting married either. Too many emotions were pounding away inside of me, and I knew I was only seconds from not being able to function at all. Blood pounded in my ears, my breath caught in my throat, and gathering tears blinded me.

I turned my back on Jack and sat the coffee cup down with more control than I knew I had. And then walked out of the room to the sound of Jack's voice calling at my back.

6

THE MID-AFTERNOON SUNLIGHT BEAT DOWN THROUGH THE windows in the upstairs bedroom Jack and I shared—the same bedroom we'd made love in only hours before.

I stripped out of my clothes and tossed them into the hamper. The cloying smell of death and my lab still clung to them, though I hardly noticed. My movements were mechanical as I got into the shower and turned on the hot water. I stood with my hands braced against the wall and let the spray hit me in the face.

Something horrible built and built inside of me until there was no choice but for it to break free. The sound that escaped my throat wasn't human and I pounded my fist against the wall in frustration. I couldn't even scream right. Choked sobs took me to my knees and I curled into a ball, letting the hot water pulse against my back.

I didn't know what was wrong with me. I'd never had to deal with this loss of control before. I'd always been the type of person to know exactly what I wanted and then I went for it. I didn't let emotions get in the way of my personal goals. I had friends and lovers, a career I'd worked hard for, and a family I didn't understand—but I assumed that was normal for everyone. It didn't mean I didn't love them or wouldn't give them a kidney if they'd asked for one. They were my family.

But there were all types of families. Jack, Vaughn, Dickie, and Eddie had been both my family and my friends. Things had changed between us over the years—as marriages, divorces, relationships, and children had taken root. But we were still family. Only now I didn't feel as if I really belonged anymore. Didn't feel as if I belonged anywhere really.

I don't know how long I stayed on the shower floor, but the water turned cold and I shivered beneath the icy spray. I reached up blindly to turn the faucet off and dragged myself to a standing position by using the towel bar to support myself.

I half-heartedly dried my hair and wrapped the towel around me, and then I stumbled into the bedroom and fell face first onto the bed. I was asleep before my head hit the pillow.

————

"WAKE UP, Jaye. We've got to move."

Jack's exact words barely cut through my sluggish brain, but I heard the urgency in them. I'd spent too many years as an ER doctor to not be able to spring out of bed and pull on clothes before my brain was fully functional. In fact, as I did so now I was reminded of those days.

I had on clean jeans and a lightweight black sweater before I asked Jack what the emergency was.

"What's wrong?" My voice was hoarse—barely discernable —from the crying jag I'd had earlier and Jack looked at me sharply. My eyes were probably puffy too so I kept my gaze averted and slipped on black boots. I headed down the stairs and grabbed my medical bag, and I heard Jack's footsteps behind me.

"We've got a mess on our hands. Ben Carver just called me." Jack took the keys from my hand and he instead led me to his police cruiser. Whatever was going on he wanted to have an official presence.

"If there's a body I need the Suburban. I can follow you to the scene."

"There's no body." He didn't say anything else until I was seated in the passenger seat of his cruiser and belted in. He hit the sirens, did a U-turn, and sped out of the long driveway and onto the main road. There was still tension between us and my hands were clasped on the handle of my medical bag so my knuckles were white with strain.

"What did Ben want?"

"Colburn ran the prints we took today, and when they went through the system they sent up all kinds of red flags. Carver was giving us a courtesy call to let us know we're going to have the FBI breathing down our neck in the next few minutes."

I jerked in my seat and had the urge to jump out of the car and run back to the house so I could hide the boxes we'd left out on the table.

"I put them in the safe," Jack said, and I relaxed a little. "I warned Colburn to be ready for them and to cooperate, but I thought you'd want to be there when they serve the warrant to retrieve the body from your lab."

"Warrant? Are they going to search the whole premises?"

"No, it's specific to the body and any information, materials, or samples taken from the body in the course of our initial investigation."

"You're not telling me something." I watched his jaw clench as he pressed on the brake a little. We were getting closer to town and the traffic was heavier. Most people in cities learned to get out of the way when emergency vehicles had their lights on. The people in Bloody Mary slowed their pace and gawked as much as possible while whispering speculation.

"The prints belonged to Dean Wallace. He was a SWAT officer out of DC and transferred six years ago to join the Capitol Police. He was a sergeant there and had a good record."

"Six years ago. He was one of yours?"

"Yeah. He was one of mine." Jack hit his hand against the steering wheel in a rare showing of temper.

The late afternoon sun was a flaming ball of orange in the sky and it glared through the windshield as we turned onto Catherine of Aragon. Jack turned the sirens off but left his lights flashing as he parked the cruiser at an angle in the driveway.

"Tell Carver I owe him one," I said, looking at the fleet of black SUVs that pulled up seconds after us.

"You can tell him yourself. He'll be here a little later to check on things."

"What exactly does Carver do at the FBI?"

"Nobody knows. But he's a good friend to have in our corner. Let's go get this over with. The easier we make things for them the less complicated it will be."

"They'll have run my background before they got here." I wiped my sweaty palms on my jeans and reached for the door handle.

"Yeah. They'll have done a full background. We'll deal with that too." His voice was strained and he didn't reach out to soothe me like he normally would have. He was still angry. Still hurt I hadn't confided in him.

I hadn't realized how much I'd gotten used to his touch—a squeeze of the hand or the way he always ran his hand down the back of my hair. I felt the absence of it now.

I stepped out of the car and my boots scraped across the driveway as I moved to stand next to Jack. A squat rectangular building sat across the street. It had once housed a variety of businesses, but the economy had hit the area hard and the only thing left was a Laundromat. I recognized Molly Beamis and Lena Rodriguez as they lost interest in their laundry and came out to stand on the sidewalk to watch.

I felt their gazes boring into me, and when they started whispering to each other behind their hands, I knew they were thinking the FBI was back for me. If that rumor got out it would be bad for business, and business was already bad enough as it was. I sighed as I watched Molly dig her cell phone out of her pocket and make a phone call. The whole town would be out watching the show before too long.

We waited as the doors of the black SUVs seemed to open in tandem. A man in a black suit with a thin black tie took the lead and headed in our direction. He pulled off his sunglasses and hooked them in the front pocket of his jacket.

"You must be Sheriff Lawson," he said, extending a hand. "I'm Special Agent Greer. You have good contacts. We've barely had the warrant for an hour, and it took us about that long to get here."

Greer was probably late forties with thinning brown hair and intelligent hazel eyes. He was trim and was a couple of inches taller than me.

"An hour's a long time in this business," Jack said. "This is Doctor Graves."

I shook hands with Agent Greer.

"If you'll go ahead and open up for us we'll be out of your way sooner rather than later," he said.

"Are you just retrieving or are we going to be here a while?" Jack asked before I could answer Greer.

Greer's eyes were shrewd as he stared hard at Jack. "You've got an impressive record, Lawson. Good experience and leadership qualities. What are you doing wasting your time here?"

"I take it that's the non-answer way of saying we're going to be here a while."

"After you, Doctor Graves," Greer said.

"Sure." I started to move away from Jack and let the team assembled at the door inside, but Jack stopped me with a touch on the arm and then he immediately dropped his hand back to his side.

"Just so we keep everything nice and tidy, I need to see the warrant."

"Of course." Greer turned and gestured to the SUV he'd gotten out of and the passenger door opened. The first thing I saw were bronze heels attached to an endless amount of legs.

I felt Jack stiffen beside me and turned to look at him, but his face was impassive as ever. I looked back at the woman and had one of those moments of utter and complete jealousy. Not because of the way all of the men in the vicinity had stopped and directed their attention solely at her, but because she was just one of those naturally beautiful women who commanded her sexuality and used it to get exactly what she wanted.

Blond hair shimmered under the setting sun, and it fell in waves around her shoulders. Her cheekbones were high and her skin pale and flawless. Her lips were crimson and she smiled smugly as she walked over the uneven ground with a smooth glide that should have been impossible. As she drew closer I saw the tiny mole just above the corner of her lip and caught myself before I rolled my eyes.

Her suit was the same tasteful bronze as her shoes. The pencil skirt fitted so it showed off those million dollar legs. The matching jacket was buttoned, showcasing a tiny waist and just a hint of cleavage.

When she reached us she handed the warrant over to Agent Greer and then he handed it to me. I didn't look at it because the woman hadn't taken her eyes off Jack during the entire spectacle.

"It's been a long time, Jack," she said, pouting prettily. "Aren't you going to say hello?"

I felt more than heard Jack's sigh.

"Hello, Lauren."

7

"THIS IS LAUREN RHODES," AGENT GREER SAID, SINCE IT was obvious introductions weren't needed for anyone but me. "She's an attorney with the Department of Justice. Lauren, this is Doctor Graves."

Lauren's clear blue eyes met mine and she gave a professional nod. "If you'll look over the warrant and make sure everything is in order we can get to the bottom of this."

I opened the folded sheaf of papers with surprisingly steady hands, but I didn't really see the words on the page. The tension between Jack and Lauren was palpable and I had nothing but questions that I knew I didn't want the answers to.

"It looks good," I said, folding it back up. "Let me unlock the door for you." I turned my back on Jack and Lauren and walked swiftly up the sidewalk where the team was waiting to get in. Agent Greer stayed at my side.

I unlocked the kitchen door and tried not to panic as the team crowded in behind me. I stood in front of the keypad,

blocking the view of the code that would let us into the basement. The door opened with a soft click and the cold air
rushed over us.

"You're welcome to come down and observe while we
remove the remains," Greer said. "We have no intention of
inconveniencing you."

"Thank you."

The lights came on automatically as we stepped over the
threshold and I led them down the staircase instead of using
the elevator. I showed them the freezer where I was keeping
the body, the bag of clothing, and the sealed bag with his
finger and the removed skin I'd had to take for the
fingerprint.

I stood off in the corner as they searched every inch of the lab
and every file cabinet drawer to make sure there wasn't
further information I was keeping somewhere. I don't know if
it was divine intervention or something else at play that had
made me take the boxes belonging to my parents, but I was
glad we'd moved them to Jack's.

Jack and Lauren came down through the elevator—probably
in deference to the heels that brought the top of her head even
with Jack's chin—and my gaze passed over them briefly,
even though I could feel Jack's eyes. He broke away from
Lauren and came to stand beside me, leaning back against the
wall in a casual pose. I crossed my arms over my chest and
scooted farther back into the corner. I answered questions
when they were directed at me, but mostly I was just numb.

"You don't have to stay here the whole time," Jack finally
said. "This could take hours. We could wait up in the kitchen
and make some coffee." Jack's hand came up and rested on

the back of my neck and he kissed my temple, but I was still stiff under his touch.

"I'm sorry for earlier."

I wasn't sure if he was referring to our argument or how he'd reacted to seeing Lauren, so I didn't say anything.

"I understand why you waited to tell me, but it doesn't make it hurt any less that your first reaction wasn't to confide in me but to deal with it yourself."

I sucked in a deep breath and nodded. "I don't think I can talk about this now, Jack. I'm sorry I didn't tell you, but the way you reacted says a lot, and you've made your position perfectly clear. I probably should have told you sooner. I'll apologize for that. I'm still getting used to having someone to go to."

"The thing is, Jaye, you've always come to me with personal things before. I've been your friend longer than I've been your lover. The friendship part shouldn't change now that we're sleeping together."

I pressed my lips together and pushed away from the wall. "I could use some coffee. Maybe with a shot of the whiskey I keep under the counter."

Jack said a few words to Agent Greer and then we headed back up to the kitchen. I felt Lauren's eyes follow us up, but I didn't turn to look at her. She was an element of this mess I couldn't deal with just yet.

The kitchen was surprisingly empty considering the chaos happening below, and I went automatically to the cabinet and pulled out the coffee grounds. Jack took the bag from my hands out of self-preservation because I always made shitty coffee no matter how precisely I followed the instructions.

"I need to explain about Lauren." Jack's voice was soft, but I looked around to make sure no one was standing nearby so they could overhear us.

"No, really you don't, Jack. We both had a past before this thing with us started. She isn't the first of your lovers I've met, and she probably won't be the last. Just like I'm sure you've run into mine. It's a small world."

Jack scowled and took mugs down from the cabinet at the mention of previous lovers. "I know you're angry at me, but there's no reason to take cheap shots. Lauren and I were together a long time ago."

He poured the coffee, and then bent down to the bottom cabinet to pull the bottle of Jameson's I kept there in case of emergency. He poured a healthy dollop into each coffee mug and then handed me one.

"And like I said, I don't need to hear the details, but it was obvious to everyone standing outside that there was something between the two of you, and neither of you bothered to try and hide it. Just drop it, Jack. I can only deal with one fight at a time. You're the one who called off your "vacation.""

We sat side by side on the stools that pulled up to the large square butcher block island that sat in the middle of the kitchen, and the tension roiled off both of us in waves. We weren't there very long before heavy footsteps echoed on the stairway and Agent Greer came through the door.

"They're finishing up and are ready to transport," he said, eyeing the coffee.

"Would you like a cup?" I asked.

"If you don't mind. There are a few things we need to talk about, Sheriff Lawson. Doctor Graves can stay if you wish, otherwise we can take this to your office and handle this there."

I looked back and forth between Jack and Agent Greer and I couldn't interpret whatever silent communication was happening between them.

"I don't understand." I put Greer's cup in front of him and took my seat beside Jack. "What does any of this have to do with Jack?"

"Because Dean Wallace was one of mine. And I'm going to assume there's more to this than just collecting his body and getting out of our way."

I heard the clank of the elevator and more footsteps on the stairs, and the body was taken out of the kitchen and out to one of the waiting SUVs. They all moved with an eerie silence as if they didn't need words to communicate.

"You'd be right about that," Greer said, pulling a thick file from his briefcase. "Staying or going, Doctor Graves?"

"She stays," Jack said. "We're engaged to be married."

Lauren Rhodes made an appearance at the top of the basement stairs at that point and I saw the surprise on her face before she quickly masked it and moved to the barstool beside Agent Greer.

The air expelled from my chest at the news that Jack still planned to marry me, and my grip tightened on my coffee cup as I tried to get hold of my emotions. I knew a woman like

Lauren—a woman that saw something she wanted—would exploit whatever weakness she could find until she achieved her goal.

"Congratulations," Greer said. "I didn't find that information in your file."

Lauren's eyes cut to my vacant ring finger and I didn't have to interpret the arched eyebrow before she turned her attention to Jack.

"We just got the details worked out today. It took me a while to talk her into it," Jack said, his mouth quirking. "She's stubborn." Jack gave all pretense that he was relaxed and in a good mood, and it would fool anyone but me, but I could see the tension. I wasn't that good an actress, so I spent most of the time with the coffee cup held in front of my face and the scent of whiskey tickling my nostrils.

I felt bad for not offering Lauren a cup of coffee, so I offered to get her some.

"I don't drink coffee, but I'll take water if you have it."

I decided I might as well try to be friendly. I just wanted the night to be over. "God, how do you survive without coffee?"

"It makes me jittery, but I practically live on Diet Coke."

I handed her the bottle of water I'd taken from the fridge, but I was distracted by the photographs Agent Greer was lining up on the table. Crime scene photographs taken from somewhere, a mass killing by the looks of things.

"Six years ago, a seven-man team attempted a heist on the Federal Reserve Bank in Washington DC. From the intel gathered, we know they had a top notch electronics guy, someone working inside the bank, a cop, a security expert, a demolitions expert, and the money men to fund the operation."

As soon as Greer mentioned the Reserve Bank heist I took Jack's hand in my own and held tight—the anger between us forgotten for the moment. I knew that had been his last mission as a SWAT cop and all I knew after that was it had taken him months to heal from the wounds.

"The team went in just at closing," Greer continued. "The bank guards were all killed instantly and twelve employees were executed. They didn't need help getting past the vault security because whoever was running the electronics knew the system and managed to hack past all the government walls that had been built up."

"SWAT was immediately called to service and a ten-man unit went in the Reserve building with only one goal—to eliminate the threat. You were the Commander, Sheriff Lawson."

"You're not telling me anything I don't already know. I think my memory is probably better than whatever you have there in your notes." Jack's voice was steady and he looked Greer straight in the eyes. "What your file doesn't mention is the stench of fresh death. Of stepping over the body of a man in uniform who was curled over the body of a heavily pregnant woman, both so riddled with bullets that there was no way to step around the blood. Only through it. You have the reports. You have the photographs." He put his finger over the image he'd spoken about and pushed it back toward Greer. "I've already made my statements."

"I have what was written by the agent who initially did the investigation. I want to hear it from your own mouth."

I shot Greer a look of censure and wanted nothing more than to tell him where he should shove his request. Jack had done his time and paid a price. But Jack turned his head and looked at me, and I could see the resignation on his face. There was no way to get out of this. So he weaved his fingers tightly with mine and gave his report.

"We already had quite a bit of intel by the time we mobilized. We had accurate blueprints and we were able to see heat signals as they moved around. We knew there were no living civilians and we knew the suspects were heavily armed.

"It was a relatively fast job. We went in hot and silent, and I was the last inside because I was team leader. We broke off into two lines of five and then did our jobs. Our orders were to kill, not apprehend. As we made it farther into the building and began taking them out, my team went through our usual patterns, what we'd been trained for. We broke off into smaller groups of two and secured the areas."

"But something didn't go as planned?" Greer said.

"You could say that," Jack said wryly. "I was in front by this time and I broke off to one of the vault rooms with Detective John Elliott. He was covering my back. It was routine, but he and I picked the vault area where several of the robbers were located. They'd set explosives in some of the other areas, covering their trails, as they got ready to make an exit. Sometimes it really just comes down to luck, you know?"

"I know," Greer said, nodding.

"Elliott and I just happened to pick the right room. It wasn't even the next room on our normal rotation. I can't tell you why I zeroed in so far down the hall, but I knew I trusted my gut over procedure at that moment. If Elliott and I had gone into the room we were supposed to go in they would have been able to ship what was left of my body back in a Zip Loc baggie."

"Your partner didn't question procedure? He just followed you?"

"My team was the best there was. We trained together and socialized with each other. We were brothers. A cohesive unit. And we didn't need words or questions when we were on an op. It was like being inside of each other's minds and always being able to anticipate the next move. It was clockwork."

"So we go in and secure the corners first, and then Elliott and I are standing neck deep in the red zone. Shots are fired from both sides. I was wearing a vest, but there's a weak spot on each side. The first and second bullets were pretty close together and came in from my right side. The third hit my upper arm. The bullets broke ribs and collapsed my lung, but by that time the rest of the team had converged and the threat was eliminated."

"Detective Elliott took a bullet to the head," Greer said.

"Yes." Jack didn't elaborate. I knew the death of one of his brothers would be like losing a family member.

"When did you realize Elliott was on the take?"

Jack paused and then let out a slow breath, but he didn't take his eyes off Greer. "When he shot me three times and left me for dead."

8

MY HEAD JERKED TO LOOK AT JACK AND I STARED AT HIM open mouthed with surprise.

"You failed to put that information in your initial report," Greer said.

Jack shrugged. "He had a wife and two little girls, one of which was in the middle of experimental chemo treatments at the time. I could put two and two together. And those little girls didn't deserve to have their father taken off the pedestal they'd put him on. They would have lost both medical and widow's benefits. He and I were the only two who knew what really happened. Which leads me to ask how you got hold of that information, and it's obvious this is what you were getting to all along."

"You realize that I could have you brought up on obstruction charges. Take away your badge."

"You need me for something. Otherwise you would've already done it and I'd have kept my mouth shut. Try again."

"Your file says you have a tendency to be cocky and you have issues with authority."

"Which is why I like being the boss. In my experience, the higher up the food chain you go, the more idiots and political bullshit you run into." He turned toward Lauren and gave her a curious stare. "And why are you here? It's obviously not for my benefit."

"The Justice Department has an interest in seeing this through."

Jack raised a brow. "Interesting."

"What the hell does that mean?" I asked. "She didn't say anything."

"It means they have a dog in the fight, but she's not going to tell us what it is. Why don't you lay it out for me, Agent Greer?"

"Like you said, they would have gotten away with the robbery if you hadn't followed your gut. They had technology and equipment we'd never seen before, they moved and strategized like the military, and they had money backing the expedition. They knew the weak points beneath the building and cut a goddamned hole through the floor with a laser knife out of some sci-fi movie, and they had ATVs waiting below to transport them through the underground sewer system quickly."

"They had the building set with enough explosives to turn it to dust once they'd escaped past the hot zone. They had money and power and talent for the job, and you and your team took every one of them out. At least the body counts we came up with on sight corroborated with the statements you and your team gave. But we think we maybe missed someone."

"Seven men, seven bodies recovered," Jack said. "Who could we have missed?"

"You tell me." Greer took more photographs out of his bag and laid them side-by-side across the island tabletop—nine photographs all together.

"Jesus," Jack whispered, his voice sounding as broken as mine. He stood up and leaned over the photos, touching each one reverently.

Each photograph showed a body in various states of decomp. I tried to look at them as a coroner, as an outsider, and piece together what they all had in common. One man had been garroted. Another had his throat slit. Some had been exposed to the elements for long periods of time before their bodies had been discovered and documented. Nine men were dead whoever they were.

"Winters, Gonzales, Price, Dreyer, Thompson, Garfield, Caine, Wolfe, and Santos. They all have names, Agent Greer. They're not just crime scene photographs."

"Goddammit!" Jack hefted the bar stool with one hand and threw it with all his might to the other side of the kitchen, knocking a clock from the wall and chipping the doorframe. He turned away from us and braced his hands against the kitchen counter, keeping his head down as he tried to get himself under control. His back and arms were stiff and his fingers bit into the Formica.

I hadn't seen Jack lose his temper like this in more than a dozen years. He kept a tight rein on it normally, and I knew there was nothing to do but wait it out and let him cool off. Lauren started to open her mouth, to say something to him, and I shook my head. She wisely shut her mouth and left him alone.

"Wallace was number ten," Jack finally said.

Greer nodded. "And Elliott was eleven. Or one if you want to be technical."

"So that makes me twelve."

I realized then who the men in the photographs were, and a fear so sharp and sudden came over me that I almost doubled over. It was nothing like the fear I'd experienced for myself over the last months. It was fear for a man I loved more than life itself—a man who made me a better person—who made me whole.

"Why isn't he under protection?" I asked Greer, coming to my feet.

"He had to make sure I wasn't responsible first." Jack came back to stand beside me. "I'm the last man standing."

"When was the last time you had contact with any of your men?" Greer asked.

"This is ridiculous," I said, a cold fury taking root inside of me. "He could be a target and you're sitting there treating him like he's responsible."

"He covered for John Elliott. On record. There could be more he's hiding."

"Maybe you need to have an attorney present," I said to Jack.

He ran his hand down the back of my hair and squeezed my

neck. "No, it's fine, Jaye. These are questions that have to be asked. And bringing a lawyer into it will only slow things down with red tape and bullshit when whoever did this to my men needs to be caught and punished."

"I think I'm insulted," Lauren said. "But I agree with Dr. Graves. You need to protect yourself. I'd advise you to contact your attorney."

I could see the frustration in Greer's eyes at the suggestion, but he didn't reprimand Lauren for speaking out of turn.

"We got together once a year for a weekend the first couple of years," Jack said, ignoring our suggestion. "Winters, Dreyer, and Price transferred to different cities after the heist. Gonzales retired and opened his own consulting firm. Thompson took a slower paced job in some bayou town in Louisiana. Wallace took the job with Capitol Police. Wolfe became a high level P.I. The rest of the guys stayed on the team under a new commander."

"After about year three we weren't able to get together as much. Lives got busier. Some had gotten married and others had started families. We'd stay in touch through email and talk of all of us getting together again, but then things started getting busy for me over the last few months and that's been my focus."

"When was the last time you had contact with any of them?"

"I got an email from Price before Christmas, telling me he and his wife were expecting their first child." He touched the photo of the man I assumed was Price.

"Where did Price transfer to?" I asked.

"New Orleans."

"This crime scene isn't too old." Price was one of the men who'd had his throat slit from ear to ear. "See the way the skin at the edge of the wound is crusted? It's frozen. Dressed in a suit and tie."

"The last place anyone saw him was at end of shift. New Orleans detectives are required to wear a tie most of the time."

"He hadn't even had the chance to loosen it before this happened," I said, noting the crisp knot.

"I heard from Winters' wife when he died in that car accident in January," Jack said. "I was able to make it out for the funeral, and most of the guys were there too, but since you've got Winters here in your lineup I'm assuming the crash wasn't an accident."

"Not an accident," Greer confirmed.

"What about Dreyer? Was he the first?"

"Who's Dreyer?" I asked, and Jack pointed to the photograph.

"Yes, we believe Dreyer was the first victim," Greer confirmed. "He transferred to SWAT in Texas. He always took a couple weeks vacation during hunting season every year. He's got no family still living and never married, so no one missed him when he didn't check in. He was hit with a long range rifle right through the heart."

I looked at the photograph in question and grimaced. The bullet hole was neat and round and the blackness of old blood was visible on the required blazing orange vest that would make him visible to other hunters. But Dreyer hadn't been found for a long time and the animals had scavenged on him. It wasn't a pretty sight.

"When he didn't report back to work, a search party was sent out. You can see by the area that this wasn't the kill site. The body was dragged and buried under some leaves behind some rocks. It took them two more days to find him after the alert went out. The local police department interviewed everyone who'd checked in and out during that time but didn't find anyone who clicked. The case is still open but cold. They have no leads or even a hint of a suspect. It's noted in the file that the investigating officer thinks the killer was never registered at the hunting lodge. The land where they're allowed to hunt backs up to private property and they found some ATV tracks along the fence line, but there's no telling who they belong to or how long they've been there."

"I wasn't able to make it to his funeral," Jack said. "I was in the middle of an investigation and we had our own killer on the loose."

"Winters was next in January. He lost control on icy roads and went over the bridge into the water. One of the witnesses on the scene thought she might have seen another car nudge him so he lost control, but she couldn't be sure. And another witness swore he didn't see any other cars on the road. No one could get him out of the water until rescue came because the water was so cold."

"February and March were quiet. Then two weeks ago your men were hit starting every couple of days. At first no one put it together. Not until Santos was killed. He was number five, and I don't even think the FBI would have been involved if the body hadn't been found on federal property. The killer made a mistake there because there was no reason to tie the other deaths in at that point. Five cops in different states with different specialties—the only thing connecting them being the SWAT team they belonged to six years prior. By the time I had all the information, Caine and Gonzales were dead. I put light surveillance on you, Wallace, and Wolfe, both for protection and to see if either of you had flipped your lids and were going after your old squad mates."

"Tell Agent Donaldson he needs to do a better job of going unnoticed," Jack said. "I had him made after he'd been in town for five minutes. I just wasn't quite sure what he was here for so I didn't blow his cover. If you'd been another day in coming though I would've had the information on my own."

Greer's eyes held respect and shrewdness as he tried to stare down Jack, not an easy thing to do considering Jack's size and the fact he intimidated most people. "I'll make sure to let him know."

"How did Wolfe and Wallace get taken out if you had eyes on them?" I asked.

"We haven't actually found Wolfe's body yet. We just know he hasn't showed up to his office or his apartment in the last four days. The apartment was clean. No sign of intrusion. Same thing with his office. He's got a steady girlfriend, but she hasn't seen or heard from him. She's the one who called it in."

"Wallace is a different story. Definitely signs of a struggle. He clocked out from shift at four in the afternoon. As best we can tell, he did a couple of errands—grocery store, dry cleaners—that kind of thing. Then he went home, changed out of his uniform and into daywear, and then he spread out his open case files on his desk and started working. It looks like he had dinner alone—a couple of beer bottles and one of those T.V. dinners found in the trash. Went to bed alone."

"He had good security, and he had damned good instincts according to his superiors and what I read in his file. The alarm had been tampered with and there were forced entry marks on both the front and back door."

"Surround and attack," Jack said. "Multiple killers."

"It looks like it, yes. Hired more than likely. Wallace put up a fight. Broken lamps and furniture. Some blood found on the scene. They'd have to incapacitate him before they removed him from the house and into a waiting car. No neighbors heard or saw anything suspicious."

"We found evidence of another crime scene near the 14th Street Bridge. Blood and brain matter consistent with two shots to the back of the head. It looks like he was tossed into the river at that point. No one saw or heard anything there either."

"These killers have worked their way from location to location, steadily traveling east, until they got to DC," Jack said. "They're trained. Professionals. And they wouldn't be traveling together, but they've worked together before. It's gone too smoothly for them not to have. They've saved me for last."

"You were the commander. It probably seems fitting to end it that way."

"I haven't seen or felt anyone else in the area that doesn't belong except for your guy."

And except for my father. I met Jack's eyes and I could tell the thought had already crossed his mind. Apparently my father was good enough at what he did to slip by Jack.

"Whoever is pulling the strings is probably waiting until some of the heat dies down. Doesn't make sense to try and take you out while you're surrounded by feds. You've put in for vacation time too, so maybe he wants to wait and see how your routine changes. See where you go. You might present them with a better opportunity."

I didn't want to think about all the opportunities Jack had probably presented the killers already. It was just sheer luck that they picked him last.

My cell phone rang and it took me a minute to remember which pocket I'd put it in. I didn't even look at the caller ID but instead switched it to silent. The ringing started again, but this time from my office.

"You need to get it," Jack said.

"Yeah, I need to get it."

"I won't go anywhere. I promise. We'll figure this out."

I nodded and stepped over the bar stool he'd thrown, and then I ran the rest of the way down the short hall to my office. I barely got there in time to take the call.

"Doctor Graves," I said, only panting slightly.

"This is Doctor Perkins at Augusta General. The Mosely family has requested you for pick up."

"Oh, no," I said, dropping back into my chair. "She was doing so well. I thought she was going to pull through."

"We all did." The doctor's voice was tired and sad.

"I'm on my way now. Give me half an hour."

"We'll be waiting."

I hung up the phone and stared blankly for a few minutes before I shook myself out of it. Leanne Mosely was a forty-year-old mother of four who'd been diagnosed with breast cancer only a few short months ago. She was active in the PTA and volunteered at the church a lot. They'd caught the cancer late because it hadn't been easily detectable, but the doctors were positive a double mastectomy and treatment would be enough. She'd had the mastectomy and things had looked good at first, but they hadn't gotten all of it. I didn't think anyone really believed it would come to this. Her oldest child was nine and her youngest was three. Devastating to say the least.

I went back down the hall in a daze and was almost inside the door before I heard the lowered voices. I probably wouldn't have even noticed if they hadn't been making an obvious effort to keep things quiet.

"Six years is a long time, Lauren. Things change. People change."

"You can tell yourself that, Jack, but people don't change that much. You're not meant for this, wasting your brain and your talent in some small town. Don't forget I know you well."

"You *knew* me well. And even then you didn't know all of me. I'm not the same person I was then."

"You could come back, you know. You left your doctoral work right in the middle. You could finish and get any number of high profile jobs."

My gut tightened and I tried to swallow. Jack had talked

about continuing his education, but he'd never told me he'd started the program.

"I thought you'd come back," Lauren said. "After you'd healed. I wanted to be with you, but every time I came you told me this was something you had to do by yourself, so eventually I stopped trying."

"I'm sorry for that. I didn't handle it right. Didn't handle a lot of things right during that time."

"I loved you. And if you hadn't been shot, it would be you and I making plans for our future."

I heard Jack's sigh and I rested my head against the faded wallpaper.

"You can't know that, and I'm not altogether sure we would be. And there's no point in this, Lauren. The past is the past."

"Come back with me," she said. "We can pick up where we left off."

"I can't do that."

"Because of her?"

"Because of her. She's my future."

"If you marry her, there's no going back. You'll be under the microscope just as much as she is. You'll never have the chance for a high profile position or a spot in the agency. She's the daughter of felons and it's never been proven without a reasonable doubt that she wasn't involved in their operation."

"You don't want to go there," Jack growled.

"Her whole family is a con. Are you a hundred percent sure

that she loves you as much as you love her? Would she protect you at all costs? If she did, she'd know that marrying you was the worst thing she could do for you and she'd back away."

"That's enough, Lauren." Jack sounded tired.

Her voice grew softer and I had to strain to hear. "I just don't want you to get hurt. I still care about you."

I couldn't stand to listen anymore and I needed to escape as soon as possible. I needed to tend to Leanne Mosely and lose myself in work. I slipped back into the kitchen and my gaze immediately went to Lauren's hand, which rested on top of Jack's in an intimate gesture. Jack pulled his hand away, and I didn't make eye contact with either of them as I went to get my bag from the counter.

"Jaye, I—"

"I've got to do a hospital pickup," I interrupted. I headed to the fridge and got out a bottle of water and resisted the urge to hold it to my forehead.

"Who?" Jack asked.

"Leanne Mosely."

"Hell. I'll go with you."

"No need. It'll be a quick trip, and you probably don't need to be out and about with a killer on the loose. Where's Agent Greer?" I still hadn't managed to meet Jack's eyes and I had a hand on the doorknob when I asked the question.

"He went outside to speak to another agent and get all the case files for me. I asked him for copies of everything so I could work this from my end too."

I finally managed to work up the courage to turn and look at Jack face to face. I couldn't play poker as well as Jack, but I knew how to blank my face when I needed to, how to pretend nothing was wrong.

"That's good," I said. "Will you have protection?"

"There will be agents in the area, but I refuse to have someone inside our home tripping under our feet all the time. I was adamant about that."

"I'll need to start on Leanne tonight, so it could be late before I get home. Be careful."

I gave Lauren a cool look and then stepped outside into the fresh air. It wasn't until I stood there a moment that I realized I didn't have my Suburban.

9

AGENT GREER WAS SPEAKING TO ANOTHER AGENT AND I stood on the steps, watching them for a couple of minutes until they looked my direction. Greer had a box of what I assumed were case files in his hand.

"Problem, Doctor Graves?"

"I've got to head to the hospital and pick up a body, but I left my Suburban at home. Do me a favor and tell Jack I borrowed his cruiser."

"No need. I can have Agent Donaldson take you to your vehicle."

"So that's Agent Donaldson?" I said, glancing at the man behind the wheel of one of the multitude of black SUVs. He looked uncomfortable and a little pissed off.

"It's good to know not everyone can recognize him." Greer sighed and shook his head in disgust.

"Jack's very good at what he does. And what he did."

"I know that better than you think, Doctor Graves. His file is impressive and his intelligence is top level. If he played by the rules a little better I'd be trying to recruit him for the FBI."

"I mean to say that I know that Jack is strong and smart and has the kind of intuition that can be unnerving, especially when he can read people so well. But this time is different."

He looked at me with a steady gaze and he finally nodded his head in agreement. "Yeah, it's different this time."

"I'm scared for him, though he won't appreciate me saying so."

"We're going to do our best to keep him safe. I've got men out all over the county and I've got my team right here digging into the files so we can have a better picture of who's doing this."

"Don't feed me departmental bullshit, Agent Greer. It took me about two seconds to realize that you have every intention of using Jack to draw out who's doing this. You've read Jack's files and probably have them all memorized, but you don't know *him*. He's one of the best men I know. Your files won't say that. And he'll put himself on the line because it's the right thing to do and because he believes his men need justice. He's carrying the weight of guilt on his shoulders right now, that there's something important he missed six years ago that could've prevented all this."

"All I'm asking is that you remember the man and not the file when you use him as the sacrificial lamb." I took a step closer so Greer had to readjust the box he held. We were almost eye-to-eye and that was good enough. "If anything happens to him I'll hunt you down. You know my background. My family. I could make it happen, and I can see in your eyes you know I'm telling the truth."

"Threatening a Federal agent isn't a good way to start our working relationship, Doctor Graves. All it will do is get you arrested."

"If anything happens to Jack, it'll be worth it. We're getting married in a couple of weeks." I moved aside and headed toward Agent Donaldson and the SUV. "It's your job to make sure he makes it to the wedding alive. Thanks for the ride."

———

IT DIDN'T TAKE LONG to retrieve Leanne Mosely's body once Agent Donaldson dropped me back at the house to get the Suburban.

All of the family had left except for Leanne's husband, Mark, by the time I arrived. And to be honest, I was thankful to not have to see the grief on her children's faces. It was hard enough looking at Mark, his face sunken and aged, and the devastation in his eyes unbearable to witness.

Death had always been a part of my life. It was always there, lurking in the corners of my mind, even when I was entrenched in life. But that didn't mean I didn't question it— didn't wonder and speculate about what happened after.

I know better than anyone the cycle of life. What happens to flesh after we draw our last breath. How the organs and tissues break down, rendering us back to dust. Death is powerful. No one is immune. And it's the living who must make their peace with it, because the dead don't give a shit.

I made an appointment to meet with Mark in the morning,

promising to take good care of his wife. I told him to go home and be with his children, and I told him how sorry I was. But I'm not sure he was really listening. He just stared as we loaded her up and I drove away.

By the time I got back to the funeral home it was well after dark and the businesses in town were long shut down. The porch lights were on; so was the light near the kitchen door where I brought bodies in and out. Jack's cruiser was gone, as well as all but one of the black SUVs.

I saw Agent Donaldson sitting across the street. He still looked pissed, so I had to figure he was being punished by given the duty of watching me. I tried not to worry about Jack and if he made it home okay. I also tried not to worry about whether Lauren had given him a ride and if they'd talked more about their past in my absence. Oddly enough, that was harder of the two to block out of my head at the moment.

I went over to Agent Donaldson and he rolled down the window.

"Is everyone gone?" I asked.

"They left about an hour ago. I'll be here to follow you home when you're ready to leave."

"I'll probably be a couple of hours at least, but thanks for waiting."

He nodded and rolled his window back up, so I guessed that meant I was dismissed. I didn't bother asking him for help with the body. It was more difficult on my own, but I'd done it before and could do it again. The most difficult part was making sure the stretcher didn't tip as I pulled it out of the back of the Suburban.

Leanne's decreased weight from her sickness made things easier and I got her out and up the ramp with little hassle. I went through the ritual of unlocking the lab door and moving her to the elevator, and I made sure to pull the door shut behind me. It locked automatically, but there was a deadbolt from the inside my parents had installed when it had been their lab.

The elevator was old and creaky and it took time to get to the bottom floor. The doors slid open and there sat my father, big as life, in a chair with his back to the wall.

"Jesus Christ, Dad," I shrieked, holding a hand to my pounding chest. He looked amused and stood slowly, sticking his hands in his pockets. He was dressed similarly to the way he'd been dressed the day before. His clothes were pressed and clean, and he was smoothly shaven.

"Are you out of your mind? The FBI is sitting right outside."

"Hmm, I know." He came over to help me pull the stretcher from the elevator and I was so surprised I let him. "Agent Donaldson needs seasoning yet. And of course I'm just very good."

It was odd working in tandem with my father once again. We hadn't done this since I'd been in high school, helping out on the weekends when I was needed. A morbid youth if ever there was one. We lifted the black bag from the stretcher to the sterile metal table I used for embalming.

My teeth wanted to chatter from either the cold or the sight of my father again, so I went and grabbed a thick sweatshirt from a hook on the wall and one of the white disposable gowns to put over my clothes.

"You need any help?"

"Why, do you have something you need to smuggle out through her body?"

"I suppose I deserve that."

"And much more. Jack knows you're in town."

"He's got his own problems to worry about. I don't think he's going to have time to actively search for me."

My head snapped up. "You don't have anything to do with the deaths of Jack's men, do you? Please tell me you don't have any part in that."

"It's not me. I could probably dig around some and help find the source."

I snorted out a laugh before I could help it. "Yeah, I'm sure that would go over well. Not to mention I'm sure you never do anything that doesn't further your own agenda."

"That's not true. You're my daughter. If you asked for help I'd give it. But you were always too damned independent to ask for your mother's and my help."

"And law abiding," I said dryly. "Speaking of, where is Mom? I'm assuming she survived the fiery crash over the side of the mountain with you?"

"Yes, but she didn't survive Kaliningrad." His voice went hoarse and he cleared it once. "We had some problems there."

I took in a deep breath and focused on setting up my equipment. She'd been dead for two years. At least to me. It shouldn't make the hurt fresh again to hear she was gone for real, but it did.

"Who's in the bag?" he asked.

"Leanne Mosely. Age forty. Cancer."

"I remember her. Your mother and I were friends with her in-laws once."

"I don't think they'd invite you to any neighborhood barbecues now if they knew you were alive. They still won't speak to me, much less look me in the eye when we cross each other on the street. I'm actually surprised I got the call to do the interment."

"You've had a rough go of it the past year. I'm sorry about that."

"Uh, huh. More likely sorry you got caught."

"They still haven't caught me," he said with a half smile.

I pulled on blue latex gloves and then unzipped the black bag, stripping it away from the husk that was Leanne Mosely. I grabbed the spray bottle of disinfectant and sprayed over the eyes, nose, and mouth and her lids automatically opened.

"That used to freak you out when you were a kid."

"One of only many things." I poured soap on my hands and started rubbing out the rigor mortis from the body. "I appreciate you trying to convince me that you're sorry about what you and Mom did and the backlash it's had on me, but I'm not buying it. You've always been a great actor. And I can deduce from our previous conversation that the only reason you're still here is because you don't have the boxes. If I'd left them here you would already be gone and we wouldn't be having this nice father daughter chat."

He smiled and jingled the change in his pockets. "Maybe. Did you go through the boxes?"

"You mean did I see all the evidence you compiled about my real parents and how you kidnapped me and forged documents so it would look like I was your own? Yes, I saw all that. Hand me the pliers there."

Anger simmered inside of me but my hands were steady as I stapled the mouth closed and stuffed the inside with cotton, giving Leeann a little fullness back in her face like she had before she'd gotten so sick.

"I don't see why you're so angry. You would have been an orphan abandoned in a foreign country if we hadn't taken you. Do you know what happens to American infants that don't have someone to claim them? They're sold—either into slavery or to be prepped for the sex trade."

"And I provided a good cover for whatever scheme you and Mom were caught in the middle of."

His lips twitched. "That too. But never doubt that you were ours."

I ignored him and went to work finding the carotid artery and tying it off in preparation for the embalming fluid. Her arteries were in bad shape because of all the chemo and it took me a while to find the jugular and cut it so the blood would flow out once I started the embalming process.

"You always had good hands," my dad said. "You wanted to be a doctor from the time you were a little girl."

"And look at me now."

"We always thought you'd be a surgeon. You've got the

hands for it, and you could gut and dress a fish faster than the pros when you were just a little thing."

"I liked being an ER doctor."

"If you'd liked it as much as you say you do, then nothing could have torn you away from it after our—accident."

"Except for the enormous amounts of debt I had to pay off because of your—*accident*. And insurance doesn't dole out money for double suicides."

"We had an account set up for you, but those bastard FBI agents tracked it and closed it down. Why didn't you just take the money that was in the bunker? It would have taken care of everything and given you a nice cushion too. Hey," he said as if a lightbulb just went off. "You could use it to open a practice here in Bloody Mary. If you hate the funeral home so much, close it down. I always hated it too, but you don't look a gift horse in the mouth."

"Jesus, are you for real? Unfuckingbelievable. You have no conscience."

"Of course I do. There are many things I regret over the course of my lifetime. But I have a sense of justice and loyalty and right and wrong. It's just that you don't understand them. We didn't raise you to be so closed-minded. There are always variations of many truths."

I straightened and looked straight at him. "You're a liar. A criminal. And a traitor to the government you worked for."

"I'll admit to the first. The second is debatable. And the third —well, maybe you didn't look closely at what was inside the boxes after all. The truth is seen differently through different eyes, Jericho. Which makes the truth nothing but lies."

"Stop calling me that." I rolled the kinks out of my shoulders and grabbed a myriad of pink chemicals from the shelf, mixing them together. The smell that always made Jack sick filled the room, and I was feeling a little sick myself at the moment.

"Why? It's your name. And it follows the Graves legacy."

I snorted out a laugh. "Yes, I'm sure using Biblical names for everyone in the family will be the same as greasing a few palms when you're standing outside the golden gates looking to get in. Good luck with that."

It somehow felt disrespectful to be having this conversation with my father over a woman as kind and loving as Leanne Mosely. I rolled the machine closer to the table and connected the arterial tube into the artery, and then I watched for a few seconds to make sure the blood was draining down the side trays on the table correctly.

"I need those boxes, Jaye. There are things I can't tell you about. In fact, most things it's better you never know about. I would never want to involve you in this life. But there are things at play here that are about more than just my life or your mother's death."

"Even if I wanted to give you the boxes, I couldn't now. Jack's seen them and looked inside of them. His sense of right and wrong doesn't have nearly as many shades of gray as yours does."

He sighed and jingled the change in his pockets again. "I know it. He's a good man. Better than most, and I'm glad you're happy together. Despite it all, I loved your mother a great deal. We had fun together. And we were friends. I miss her every day."

I hardened my heart against the sadness I heard in his voice. *It's just a con. Just another one of his lies to get what he wants.* I tied off the artery and inserted the tube in a different one so the left side of her body would plump up to match the right side. Embalming wasn't a long process, but it seemed like I'd been down here for hours with no escape.

"You need to go, Dad. I can't help you. And Jack is my priority at the moment. I'd just as soon not to have to bury anyone else."

The change in his pockets stopped jingling and I felt his disappointment in me. "It was worth a shot." He made his way up the stairs and I kept my eyes focused on the body in front of me so I wouldn't have to watch him leave again.

"Watch out for yourself, Jaye. Jack won't be the only one in danger through all this. He loves you, and that will make him vulnerable. No more late night visits to the funeral home by yourself. If I can get in without notice, then others can too."

I heard the deadbolt unfasten and the click of the door as it opened and closed again. When I looked up to the top of the stairs, he was gone.

10

BY THE TIME I FINISHED WITH LEANNE AND HAD HER BACK IN the cooler it was almost ten o'clock. I used the shower in the little bathroom off my office and changed into clean clothes, bagging up the ones I'd been wearing down in the lab.

I needed to go home and go to bed since I had an early morning with Mr. Mosely, but my brain wasn't as tired as the rest of me was. I couldn't get Lauren Rhodes' words out of my head. How Jack could be so much more without me. She was right. But despite it all I felt the need to be selfish for once. He was mine. Just like I was his. And he was worth fighting for.

If Jack wanted a career change or to get out of Bloody Mary, then I was okay with that as long as we were together. Lauren had another thing coming if she thought she could wiggle her way back into Jack's life.

I thought back to what she'd said—about how she'd tried to come see him over and over again while he'd been recovering from his wounds. I'd been there by his side and hadn't seen or heard a peep from her. And if Jack had told me to go away and let him deal with it on his own, I'd have told him too bad and muscled my way beside him anyway. If Lauren had loved him as much as she'd claimed, then she would have fought tooth and nail to help him through his recovery, despite what he said.

Jack's past was in the past. I trusted him unconditionally. Which wasn't easy for me to do considering. We'd work through this mess and then we'd finally get our happily ever after. We sure as hell deserved one.

I flicked off all the lights and locked up before I went out to the Suburban. Agent Donaldson was still in the exact place he was when I went inside, and I gave him a wave to let him know I was heading out.

My dad had been right about one thing. Jack and I wouldn't take unnecessary chances. No more going places alone, and if we needed an agent inside the house, then that's what we'd do.

Agent Donaldson turned right behind me into the long driveway that led to the house. I parked next to Jack's cruiser and another black SUV, and I assumed Greer was still with Jack inside. I looked around for any visible signs of human life —good or otherwise—before I got out of the car and headed inside. Donaldson was right behind me with his hand on his weapon. I wasn't sure it would make him feel better to know I had my hand on my own gun in the pocket of my windbreaker.

The front door opened before I got there, and Jack stood there with his weapon down at his side as he waited for me to come inside.

"I've got it from here," he said to Donaldson, and Jack pulled me inside and closed the door at my back.

My pulse jumped as he held me against his body, and he burrowed his face against my neck, breathing in the scent of me. I was glad I'd decided to take a shower.

"I missed you." He kissed just below my ear and chills pebbled over my flesh. He pulled back so he could look into my eyes, and then he took my mouth in a gentle touching of lips. The sweetness of it all enveloped me and I wrapped my arms tightly around his waist. His eyes never left mine and I could see the relief and worry now that I was safely in his arms.

"I'm sorry," he said again. "I don't want to fight." And then he kissed me again and took it deeper. My lids fluttered closed, suddenly heavy, my blood thrumming through my veins and awakening as his hands skimmed my breasts and followed the curves of my waist and hips.

When he pulled back I was panting and the room was spinning. "Do we have company?"

"Carver's in the office with all of the paperwork. He just got in about an hour ago and relieved Greer of bodyguard duty. Greer wasn't happy to see him, but once Carver assured him he wasn't there to take his case away, Greer backed down." He gave me another soft kiss on the forehead and then backed away. "We need to talk, Jaye. This can't fester between us. It'll only make things harder."

I nodded and took my gun out of my pocket and put it into the little safe that looked like a drawer in the sideboard in the entryway. I hung my jacket on the hat stand and followed

Jack into the kitchen. I smelled fresh coffee and immediately went to get a cup.

"Did you eat?" He already had his head in the refrigerator pulling out sandwich stuff. "Of course you didn't. And you've got a headache too. I can see it lurking there behind your eyes."

"I just need some coffee. And probably the sandwich wouldn't hurt."

He didn't say anything else until a thick sandwich and potato chips was placed in front of me. He grabbed a beer from the fridge and then took a seat.

"I need to explain about Lauren," he said. "I know you probably heard more than you wanted to this afternoon."

I grunted because my mouth was full of food, and it turned out I was hungrier than I thought. Martha's hamburger from lunch wasn't meant to stretch ten hours. I took a second to swallow and studied Jack. He looked a little uncomfortable and maybe a little nervous too.

"I heard enough," I finally said.

"We were involved for about a year before the bank heist. She'd barely finished law school and gotten a job at the district attorney's office. I had to testify in court one day about a gang killing we broke up, and she came up and introduced herself after. We dated for a while before things got more serious."

"I'm not really sure what happened or how it happened, but one day I looked up and we're all but living together. We were both overworked, and I was in the middle of my doctoral work." He looked up then and gave a halfhearted smile. "I didn't tell you about that."

"No, you didn't." I took a drink to clear my throat. "Why not?"

"Mostly because I wasn't sure I could go through with it to the end. I knew I couldn't be SWAT forever. It wears on your mind and your body after a time. But I wasn't sure after I quit the squad I could go back to being a regular cop either. So I thought if I got more schooling, maybe I could join the FBI and teach a few classes at Quantico. Or maybe I could sit as chief somewhere someday."

"You'd be good at whatever you decided to do."

He shrugged it off. "I knew when Lauren and I were together that she wasn't the one. I told you before that I've never told another woman I loved her, and it was the truth. You're the only woman I've ever said that to." His dark gaze was direct and I believed him. Hadn't doubted him really.

"You were always there in the back of my mind," he said. "Even when we were living in different states. But Lauren was comfortable, and it was nice to be able to go home to that comfort after being in the trenches at work."

"You really don't have anything to explain to me, Jack." I pushed my plate aside and touched his hand. "I understand. Just like I understand that seeing her yesterday caught you off guard and made you question whether everything she said might be true." I wove my fingers with his. "I understand *you*. But Lauren was right about what she said about me. About us."

Jack frowned and started to say something, but I cut him off.

"No, listen. She's right that you'll never be able to pick up where you left off with your career or go toward a high level position somewhere if you marry me. And I want you to know that I understand the sacrifice, and I love you all the more that you're willing to make it."

"It's not a goddamned sacrifice," he growled, and it made me smile just a little.

"I know. Which makes it even more special. You love me no matter what. And I trust you with my life, and more importantly, my heart." I looked into his eyes and kissed him softly, and the tension in his shoulders ebbed as he took it deeper— made it sweeter.

"I love you."

The words still made my heart flutter when he said them. "I love you too. But you should probably tell Lauren if she touches you again, I'm going to punch her in her perfect face."

Jack let out a surprised burst of laughter and pulled me into a hug. "I'll pass the word along. Are you headed up to bed or do you want to sit in on what Carver and I are doing for a while?"

"I'll sit in with you guys. I want to know what's going on." I took my plate to the sink and rinsed it before I loaded it in the dishwasher, and then I refilled my coffee. "Don't take any unnecessary chances with this. I'm scared for you."

"I'm more at the pissed off stage than scared. We'll find out who's behind this. Carver and Greer are damned good at their jobs, and I'm no slouch either."

"There's something I need to tell you, and I don't want you to get angry with me."

"That's always a good way to start a conversation. Does it have to do with your father?"

"You could say that."

He sat at the kitchen table in the little nook that looked out over the trees. In the daytime it was beautiful. In the dark it was unnerving, especially when there were madmen out for Jack's blood.

"Don't worry. Greer's got agents rotating the perimeter. Our home is safe. Never doubt that."

"I saw my father again tonight," I said. "When I came back to the funeral home with Leanne's body."

"Where? What did he want?" Jack was all cop now and I gave him a look until he relaxed back in his seat and stopped treating me like I was being interviewed.

"He was waiting for me inside the lab when I took the body down. He'd bypassed security."

"When was the last time you changed the code?"

"When I came back after the attack. So it hasn't been long. But I'm not sure anything could have kept him out. He's good at what he does or he wouldn't have made it as far as he has."

"He took a chance being down there when you might not have gone down alone."

"He's plugged into everything that's going on. He knew Agent Donaldson was sitting in front of the funeral home. He

knew what was going on with you. He said to let him know if
we needed any help."

"Jesus," Jack said, pushing up from the booth and getting a
cup of coffee instead of another beer. "He's got balls. I'll give
him that."

Our knees bumped as he sat back across from me. "I take it
he was there for the boxes?"

"Yeah. I let him know I'd told you he was back. He didn't
seem overly concerned."

"He knows I've got my hands full with something else at the
moment. It's actually brilliant timing on his part. And it
makes me wonder if he didn't know some of what was going
on before he decided to rise from the dead."

"I had the same thought. He said my mom is dead." I looked
down into the steaming blackness of my cup as I told him. "It
shouldn't seem so fresh. She's been dead to me for two
years."

My hands held the cup for dear life and Jack wrapped his
hands around mine. "It doesn't make the truth hurt any less."

"No, I guess not. He said they had trouble in Kaliningrad and
she didn't make it out. And he asked me if I'd looked inside
the boxes. He said his future depended on the information
that was in there."

I filled Jack in on the story my dad gave me on why they
stole me and claimed me as their own, trying to keep the
emotion out of my voice and just state the facts.

"He won't stop until he has those boxes." He was my father,
at least in name, but I couldn't help a felon and traitor pave

the way for his escape. That would blur the lines too much, and I wasn't sure Jack would ever forgive me if I did. "We need to know what's on those flash drives."

Jack nodded. "I haven't told Carver any details, but he's said he'll help if we ask him to. If the flash drives are encrypted, he'll be our best bet on breaking through. Carver would make an excellent criminal."

"In my experience, most cops would."

Jack arched a brow but didn't refute the statement. "It worries me that your dad can find you alone so easily. He knows your schedule and who you're with."

"Like I said, he's tapped into what's going on."

"I don't want you going anywhere alone until he's found. Not even to a public restroom. I don't know what his agenda is, but he can't be trusted."

It was my turn to arch a brow. "Since I know you love me to distraction, I'm going to pretend that's the reason you're giving me orders instead of asking. And I'll make you a deal. I won't be alone if you won't be alone. My father is the least of our worries for now."

He pulled back his hands and sighed, and then he scooted out from the booth to stand. I stood up after him, refusing to be the one in the less dominant position.

"You know I can't promise that, Jaye. If we find out enough information and we know his weakness, it would be procedure to exploit it. He wants me dead. And if I have to be bait, then it's something I'll do to catch this asshole and make sure he pays for what he did to those men."

"I know that, Jack. You're a damned hero." It didn't exactly come out as a compliment. "But I'm just asking you to not take unnecessary chances. We'll cross the bait bridge if and when we get to it."

He leaned against the island and the corner of his mouth twitched. "I was expecting more of an argument."

"Maybe later. It's been a long day. Besides, I worked out most of my frustration on Agent Greer. I told him we were getting married in two weeks and you'd better be there alive or there'd be hell to pay."

It wasn't often I caught Jack off guard, so it was nice to see the genuine shock on his face before a slow smile took over.

"Is that right?"

"Yeah. Is that okay?"

"That's perfect. I know we talked about eloping, but even with that there's planning involved. I suggest we pass the whole thing over to my mother to organize while we're dealing with this."

I shifted uncomfortably. "I don't want a big wedding. I thought we'd just go somewhere and sign some papers. I don't need a big ceremony or dress or anything."

"Maybe you could wear your prom dress from junior year," Jack said, waggling his eyebrows.

"You promised you'd never bring that dress up again."

"Sometimes it's hard not to. That dress is burned into my corneas for eternity."

"It would serve you right if that's what I showed up in."

"And yet, I'd marry you anyway. That should say something."

"Fine, your mother can handle whatever details need to be handled. But I'm serious about not having a big crowd of people. It would be embarrassing to show up for a wedding where everyone is sitting on the groom's side."

"How about my parents and our closest friends? Not more than ten or fifteen people. Very small and intimate. All you have to do is show up."

"Deal," I said, holding out my hand to shake on it like we were back in grade school. He took my hand and then pulled me into his embrace.

"The big kids seal it with a kiss."

"Oh, well then—" and when his lips touched mine we were both laughing.

11

"IT'S ABOUT TIME," BEN CARVER SAID ONCE JACK AND I finally made an appearance in the front office. "Some of us have been working in here instead of making out in the hallway."

"You must have eyes in the back of your head, Carver," Jack said, moving to stand in front of the two long whiteboards that took up most of the room.

Ben Carver was probably a couple of years older than Jack, and they'd been friends for a lot of years. Carver was just under six feet and stocky with it. His hair was sandy blonde and his eyes a soft green that sparkled with good humor. Laugh lines spread out from his eyes. He still wore his holster and weapon just like Jack, even though we were safe inside the house.

"Good to see you, J.J.," he said. "You just get prettier and prettier every time I see you. You ready to leave this loser and run away with me?"

"Not if you're going to bring your wife along. I like to have my men all to myself. I'm selfish that way."

His expression was deadpan but I could see the humor lurking in his eyes. "Weirdly enough, she said the same thing last time I proposed a three-way. You women are all the same."

I nodded soberly. "Heartless bitches, each and every one."

"Your man is in a mess here. I leave him alone for a few days and this is what happens."

"You're about to be in a mess once I rearrange that pretty face of yours. Now stop busting my chops and flirting with my woman."

"I'm sorry? Did you really just call me your woman?" I leaned back against the edge of Jack's desk and raised my brow.

"You're a woman. And you're mine. Thus, my woman. When we get married, I'm going to call you my wife, so you should probably be prepared for that."

"Hey," Carver said, grinning from ear to ear. "You guys are getting married? It's about damned time. Can I get an invite? Do you know how many years I've had to listen to stories about you from this lovesick fool?"

I hid my smile behind my coffee cup. "You're a good friend to my man, Carver."

"Your man?" Jack asked.

"Just trying it on for size. I figure after we're married I'll be calling you asshole instead of my husband. At least according to Martha."

"You're going to pay for that later," Jack said, tugging at the back of my hair.

"I sure as hell hope so."

"You guys are making me uncomfortable. I haven't had sex in weeks. Do you know how long you have to go without after your wife has a baby? It feels like forever and a day."

"We don't want to hear about your sex life, Carver. I feel sorry enough for your wife as it is. Let's talk about murder instead."

"My second favorite topic of conversation." Carver pointed to the long whiteboard on the left side of the room. "Jack and I were setting this all up before you got here. We've got the crime scene photos of the ten men under Jack's command, their TOD and COD listed below. Below that we have family members and financial reports. Wolfe's body hasn't been found yet, so I've got him over to the side along with all the same data."

Carver maneuvered a smaller whiteboard so it stood next to the victims. I didn't recognize the men in these photographs, but I had a feeling they were the men responsible for the heist that started this whole ball rolling.

"Seven men went inside the bank that day. One man was already on the inside—Eric Lieber. He was the bank manager and had keys and passcodes. The other five men trickled in over a period of forty-five minutes, dressed in suits and each holding a briefcase. Five o'clock came and the guard at the door locked them so no new customers could come in. At the same time, Lieber shut down the emergency security that would alert the authorities in case of robbery. He had to override it, and eventually someone would have been sent out to see if it was a glitch, but it bought them a few minutes."

"The other five men drew their weapons and started firing. They had no plans to take hostages. Their goal was to kill anyone inside and move on. But one of the victims managed to dial 911 and leave the line open while everyone was being slaughtered."

"Then we got the call and suited up," Jack said. "Even in an emergency it takes us time to coordinate. The local police cordoned off the area, not that it would've done any good with the underground escape they'd planned on using. Another fifteen minutes for us to grab our equipment and for me to brief the team on the ride over. Everyone inside was already dead and they were already finessing their way through to the vaults when we arrived."

"What do you mean finessing?" I asked. "I thought Lieber had the keys and passcodes."

"He did, but not in their entirety. No man or woman would be given access to every part of the bank. You give your trusted officials portions of the whole, just enough to get into the smaller vaults and a partial code and retinal scan for the giant vault where most of the gold was kept."

"Lieber's brother, Karl, was the computer whiz, and was able to recreate the other parts of the passcodes to get into the main vault, including forging the retinal scans of the two other members needed to open the vault. Karl Lieber was more than a genius. I've never seen or heard of technology that sophisticated before, and the Pentagon swooped in and confiscated every bit of it before it could leak. We're talking technology of the future, and we've got nothing in place to defend against it."

"You sound envious," I told Carver.

"You have no idea how badly I want to get my hands on those files." Carver blew out a breath so the hair that had fallen over his forehead fluttered. "Anyway, both Liebers were single, but they left behind grieving parents who had no idea what their children were up to. They moved to London for a while because the embarrassment was so great. Apparently they're rather well to do in the upper crust. They do still maintain a New York residence though."

"Moving on, we've got Adam Boxer. He served three tours in Afghanistan before he came back to civilian life. He had a high aptitude for chemistry and math, and so the army thought he'd be a good fit for explosives. They were right about that. While the rest of the team was killing the hostages, he was wiring the building with explosives. Very sophisticated in nature. He left behind a wife, no children. His parents are also deceased."

"Next we have Peter Anderson. Born and raised in Chelsea, he was the British partner of the security firm of Anderson Parker Security. The Parker being for Jordan Parker, who headed up the U.S. Branch. Anderson and Parker brought in the nifty gadgets used during the heist, some of which they'd created themselves, including that very awesome laser saw they used to slice through the floor like it was hot butter. There's also a childhood connection between Anderson and the Liebers."

"Then there's Martin Stark. It's just fucking dumb luck that he was caught in the fray. His day job was spent as a strategist for Wall Street, but he was better known for strategizing heists in Berlin, Dubai, Malta, and New York just to name a few. He was a master of organizing a team and teaching them how to maneuver with almost military precision. He was never caught, only suspected of the crimes, but we all know that's bullshit. The crazy thing is all of those jobs were done with a different crew—from as small as four to as large as twelve. That's unheard of, but Stark took his time in the planning. He spent years between jobs, as many as six or eight, while he trained his men and worked out logistics."

"And then there was John Elliott," Jack said. "He was the outsider they brought in. All of these other guys came from money. Stuff like this was a game to them and they kept upping the stakes. But John was desperate. His daughter was dying and he would have done anything to give her the treatment she needed, and they exploited that and probably never planned that he'd take part of the cut. Elliott was the fall guy whose body would be left behind when they made their escape."

"I never noticed anything was off." Jack touched the picture of Elliott that was a duplicate of the one on the other board that held his team. "Ever since Katie was diagnosed he was always more tense, more worried, and we hashed it out over beers a couple of times. But I never saw anything like this coming. The thing about Elliott, all my men, was when they were focused on a mission, they were stone cold. If you ever question or doubt while you're in the middle of an op then you might as well put a bullet in your brain before someone else does. The situations are too dangerous, and the lives of your brothers are on the line."

"You can't blame yourself, Jack." I rested my hand on his

lower back, hoping I could comfort him. "You couldn't have seen any of this. No one could have."

"It sure as hell doesn't feel that way."

"This was all information uncovered during the initial investigation," Carver said. "What we've got to do now is connect the dots. Try to find the thread that connects those men to whoever is killing off the SWAT team. We'll need to reinterview all the families. We'll also need to see if we can find who's been hired for the hits. Whoever's in charge isn't getting their hands dirty with the killings. They're doling out money and giving orders. But the killers are professionals. They'd have to be to take out men with that kind of training. The list shouldn't be all that long."

"Greer was going to talk to Jane Elliott tonight," Jack said, referring to Detective Elliott's wife. "I'll need to go see her tomorrow. She shouldn't have to do this by herself, and more than likely the media will be camped out on her doorstep before too long."

"What will happen to her?" I asked.

"She'll lose her widow's benefits," Carver said. "And she'll be requestioned. It'll be rough on her and her girls. What are they, eight and ten now?"

"Yeah," Jack said. "Eight and ten. Old enough to have their illusions shattered about their father and know what it means."

"Can you look over all of the autopsy reports?" Carver asked me. "You won't have the bodies, but maybe you'll see a similar killing style between the victims. That might help us narrow our search a bit. I'm going to tell you both right now that Greer and Ms. Rhodes have an agenda. You can use them to find the truth, but don't trust them. If this doesn't turn out right, they're going to need someone to blame, and you're the only one left alive to shoulder it all."

"We'll be working parallel with each other. We're going to share notes and findings and interviews, and Greer has agreed to let the two of you help with the investigation. Though between you and me, he didn't have any choice because I outrank him and could make things very difficult. You're going to owe me a room full of strippers and a case of Glen-fiddich when this is all said and done."

"If we get out of this and your wife okays the strippers, then you've got a deal," Jack said.

───────

TWO HOURS later my eyes were crossing over autopsy reports. It was past midnight, and I'd been up for almost twenty-four hours with nothing but a catnap in between.

"I'm not going to do you any good anymore," I said, stretching my arms above my head and feeling a couple of pops along my spine.

Jack and Carver were spread out at their own tables, poring over paperwork and making notes to follow up on a few things. Police work was mostly tedious, sifting through paperwork and reports—truth and lies. Every once in a while, one of them would get up and add something to one of the boards.

"I'm about done for too," Carver said, tossing down his pen. "We can start fresh in the morning."

"Do you have an appointment with Mark Mosely tomorrow?" Jack asked.

I nodded. "Eight-thirty."

"I'll go with you to the funeral home, and then we can go pay a visit to Jane Elliott. I don't want to wait too long. And maybe she'll remember something that Greer wasn't able to get out of her."

We trudged up the stairs and Carver peeled off toward the guest room. "Thanks for letting me crash here," he said. "The B&B I stayed at last time I was here creeped me out. I kept getting the feeling that old woman who runs it was spying on me and going through my things. And I think she put a sleeping pill in the hot milk she brought me every night."

I raised my brows but wasn't all that surprised by the accusation. Wanda Baker was a curious sort. Carver was lucky he didn't wake up with Wanda's single daughter lying beside him in bed.

Jack closed the bedroom door behind us and dimmed the lights. The protective coating on the floor to ceiling windows kept people from seeing in, but that didn't mean they couldn't shoot into the room at random and get lucky. Of course, since the bedroom was on the top floor they'd have to climb a tree to get a shot off.

I kicked off my shoes and stripped out of my clothes. I probably would have left them on the floor and fallen face first into bed if Jack and I weren't still at the newly living together stage. Jack was a neat freak and liked everything in its place. I put things in their place, but I wasn't in as big a hurry to put them there as Jack was.

I picked the clothes up and tossed them in the hamper and grabbed an oversized T-shirt to slip over my head while I was still vertical. I crawled under the covers and felt the mattress dip as Jack got on the other side and pulled me into his arms.

"Love you," I mumbled, and then fell asleep.

12

THE FIRST THING I NOTICED WHEN I WOKE THE NEXT MORNING was the smell of coffee. I couldn't function without it, and I held my hand out from under the covers and heard Jack chuckle as he wrapped my fingers around the cup.

I managed to take a few sips without spilling it down my front, and I slowly felt the cobwebs clear away from my mind. The second thing I noticed was the added weight on my left hand. I nearly bobbled the cup and what was left of the coffee at the sight of the ring on my finger.

"Jesus Christ, Jack. This is the Lawson ring?" A ruby the size of my thumbnail sat in a delicate antique gold setting, and tiny diamonds flashed around the ruby. It was beautiful. And terrifying. "What if I lose it? Or it falls into a body?"

"I'd say maybe we should get a chain so you can wear it around your neck so we don't have to worry about that. I wonder if any other man has heard his fiancée utter those words?"

"This is like a real ring. A grownup ring." I still hadn't

managed to take my eyes off it. My hand looked stately and official—important—when I wore this ring. I hoped I could live up to it. "I need a manicure, but I know I'd just mess it up, so I won't bother."

"A ring like that deserves some grownup attention to the man who gave it to you." Jack slid his hand beneath my nightshirt and things started to get very warm. "It might even call for special sexual favors."

"Oh, yeah?" My eyes wanted to roll back in my head as his fingers slipped beneath the cotton of my underwear. "How special?"

"I figure since you're a doctor and all, you might know more about special than the average person. I've got to tell you my expectations are pretty high."

I looked at the clock and saw he'd woken me up half an hour before I'd set my alarm to go off. Pretty sneaky.

"I need a shower." I got out of bed and headed toward the bathroom. I stripped my nightshirt over my head and looked over my shoulder to make sure I had Jack's full attention, and then I shimmied out of the underwear.

"Are you coming?" I asked.

"Not yet."

I laughed and headed into the bathroom. "I bet I can fix that. I'm a doctor after all."

"I can't argue with that logic."

———

MY MEETING with Mark Mosely didn't take long. Leanne had been very specific in what she'd wanted as far as the burial and service went, and she'd had it all planned out just in case. By the shell-shocked look on her husband's face, she'd made the right decision to take it out of his hands.

Jack and I watched as Mark drove away, and my gaze went to the white panel van parked across the street at the Laundromat. A gray Honda was parked on the side street so there was a visual of the back of the funeral home. Both cars had undercover agents in them assigned to guard duty for the day. We would all be traveling to Fairfax to pay Jane Elliott a visit.

We'd left the cruiser and my Suburban back at the house and instead driven in Jack's forest green Jeep. It rarely got used, but it was good for longer trips, rough back roads, and snow. We made a quick stop through a drive-thru coffee shop just outside of Bloody Mary and I got a bagel as well, since the special sexual favors had made me miss breakfast.

"Do you ever think about death?" I asked. "About what happens after, I mean?"

"I don't think you can do what we do and not think about it. You're thinking of Mark Mosely," he said.

"It just makes you think, you know? They were a solid unit. They loved each other. It was plain to see anytime they were together. And now he'll never be the same. How is he going to wake up every morning knowing she won't be there beside him?" Jack took my hand and I held it like a lifeline.

"I wish I had an easy answer for you. I think you and I are at a disadvantage. Death is the norm for us. And because it is, we understand how precious living a good life can be. How important it is to not take for granted that person you wake up next to every morning, or those who are closest to us. And because of that, we're more selective in who we choose to allow to get close to us."

"Do you think this is it? That the life we have here on earth is all we'll have together?"

He looked at me with a half smile on his face. "I believe that true love exists. And I believe there are souls in this world that are meant to be together in this life and anything that comes after. After all this time, I've finally got you where I want you. There's nothing in heaven or hell that could keep us apart."

I felt some of the sadness I'd been carrying around since meeting with Mark Mosely seep from my bones.

"Think of how good I'll be at the special sexual favors by the time we get to our next life."

"I guess it's a good thing I'll be dead so it doesn't kill me."

We drove the rest of the way to Fairfax in comfortable silence. Jane Elliott lived in a middle class neighborhood of brick row houses. They all had shutters and low rooflines, and paint color was the only thing to differentiate between them. The lawns were neat and well kept with hedges lined like square green boxes across the front. The street was deserted, with only the occasional car parked in a driveway since it was a workday.

Jack parked behind an older model white sedan, and I noticed the panel van with our FBI tag kept driving and parked at the end of the street in front of another house.

A woman came to the screen door and watched as Jack and I got out of the car and made our way to the house. I didn't know Jane Elliott from Adam, but I could only imagine what she was going through right now. She'd spent the last six years learning how to go on with her life and raise her children without her husband. Nursing a child who'd just lost her father through cancer treatments on top of it all. I'd always admired women who had strength, and Jane Elliott had to be up there at the top of the list.

She opened the screen door as we drew closer—a tall, willowy woman who was almost too thin in her capri pants and oversize work shirt. Her brown hair was pulled back in a ponytail and her face was void of makeup. The raw grief on her face when she looked at Jack made my throat close with emotion.

"Jack," she said. And then he folded her into his arms, his embrace gentle as she cried against him. I stood awkwardly to the side, an intruder on the moment, because the grief on Jack's face was there as well and I knew they shared a common pain for the man they'd thought they'd known.

"I don't know what's going on," she said, swiping at her eyes. "The FBI was here yesterday. They're saying awful things about John. I don't understand."

"Let's go inside," Jack said. "We'll talk it out. Just remember that you and the girls will be okay through all of this. I'm here for whatever you guys need. Whatever is said about John won't change our friendship."

She nodded a couple of times and wiped her eyes again and then seemed to see me for the first time. "I'm sorry." Her face shone with embarrassment as she opened the door for us. "I don't normally fall apart like that. I'm Jane Elliott." She held out her hand to me and I shook it.

"I'm J.J. Graves. Jack's really good at letting women fall apart on him. He gives good hugs."

Her smile was brief, but in it I saw the attractive woman she'd been before life had leeched the color from her skin and put the dark circles beneath her eyes.

We followed her into a well-kept house that smelled like lemons and whatever she had cooking in the Crock Pot on the kitchen counter.

"I sent the girls to stay with my mother for a few days until I can get a handle on all of this. They don't know yet. And honestly I'm not sure how I can tell them." She gestured to the sitting area and Jack and I took a seat on a neutral colored sofa piled with colorful pillows.

"How's Katie doing?" Jack asked.

"She's good. A normal ten year old. She's been cancer free for three years now, and all of her check ups have been good news. An Agent Greer is the one who came to see me," she said, changing the topic. "Is what he said about John true? Was he a traitor?"

Jack sighed and looked straight at Jane when he answered. "Whatever John did, you know he did it for Katie. I know that and you know that. And I don't blame him for it. You shouldn't either."

A tear escaped and she ruthlessly wiped it away. "He never said anything to me. That he was working with those other men. Agent Greer kept asking if I remembered anything, but I don't, Jack. I swear. We were so busy with Katie at the time. One hospital stay after another. And we thought we were going to lose her. I didn't pay attention whether or not John was getting phone calls at odd hours or if I'd ever seen him meeting with someone unusual. I barely remembered my name during that time."

"It's okay, Jane. Just take a deep breath. If I can do it, I'm going to try to see if the FBI will keep John's name out of the media. You and the girls shouldn't have to deal with that. And I can only imagine what it was like for you, but I need you to try hard and think of anything that maybe stuck out as unusual during that time. Names you might have overheard or phone calls. I wouldn't ask you if it wasn't important. The whole squad is dead except for me and Sam Wolfe, and he's been missing for a few days."

Her lip trembled and she bit down on it. "Agent Greer told me. He told me you were in danger. That we all could be. It's part of the reason I sent the girls away. You need to get away from all this, Jack. I couldn't bear it if something happened to you too."

"You don't have to worry about me. I'm protected. John talked about an experimental treatment for Katie, but he said insurance didn't cover it. Did Katie ever get that treatment?"

Her brow furrowed for a minute. "Of course. It's one of the reasons she's still here with us. There's an organization— Kids With Cancer—and they raise money to donate it to families who need the kind of treatment Katie did. They covered it all."

"Who did John hang out with in his off time?"

"He was at the hospital whenever he wasn't at work, but if he took personal time he hung out with someone from the team. Or he just spent it reading a book or something. You remember how much he liked to get lost in a book."

"There wasn't anyone you didn't know hanging around? Maybe a couple of phone calls that were hangups?"

"I'm sorry." She lifted her hands and let them fall back to her knees again. "I just don't remember anything. All I know is that John's dead, and we can't ask him to his face why he did all this. I don't know what to tell you, Jack."

Jack sighed and patted Jane's hand as she quietly wept.

13

WE LEFT JANE AND HER TIDY ROW HOUSE A SHORT TIME later to make the drive back to Bloody Mary. I watched the scenery pass by in a blur as thoughts rattled around in my head like marbles.

"We've got a tail," Jack said, flicking on his blinker and moving over a lane. "Just keep looking straight ahead. We don't want to spook him until our federal friends can get a license plate and a description."

I looked in the side mirror and tried to see the cars behind. The van was easy to spot a couple of lanes over and a few cars back. I didn't see the grey Honda anywhere. "Which one?"

He moved over another lane and I saw a black Jeep with oversized tires and tinted windows follow us over. He stayed back several cars in length. Jack's cell phone rang and he put it on speaker.

"You've got a tail," one of the agents following us said.

"I see him. Can you get a license plate?"

"Negative. He's keeping a car between us and the windows are too dark to get a visual on the driver. I'm about to get off at the exit and Agent Carlson will move in. I'll pick you up about a mile down the road."

"Let me see if I can help you out some." Jack disconnected and sped up, putting distance between our tail and us. I had a white knuckled grip on the door with my right hand, and my left reached out and slapped the dash as we squeezed between a semi and a minivan. He slammed on the brakes and I jerked against my seatbelt, while the semi laid on the horn.

"There we go," he said. "What are you going to do now?"

Jack somehow managed to watch the road, the car in front of us that was so close our bumpers were almost touching, the black Jeep, and Agent Carlson, who'd just made an appearance coming up from the access road and closing in to the right of the Jeep.

My heart slammed in my chest and I watched out of the side mirror as Agent Carlson moved the grey Honda over another lane so he rode parallel with the black Jeep.

"That ought to do it," Jack said. He zipped out from between the semi and the minivan and then got off at the last second at the next off ramp.

"I think I'm going to throw up," I said.

"Nah, you're fine. You just got the wind knocked out of you when you hit the seatbelt."

The phone rang again. "Did you get it?" Jack asked by way of greeting.

"Got the license plate number, but we lost the car. When Agent Braddock came up to get in position again the driver did some maneuvering of his own and did a u-turn across the median. We decided to stick with you in case it was a diversionary tactic for someone wanting to take a shot at you."

"Did you run the plates?"

"They're registered to Walter and Megan Cockrill in McClean. The plates are supposed to be on a 2010 Range Rover. We've alerted Agent Greer. He'd like you to meet him at your office."

"Will do."

"Do you think he was right? That the driver was trying to cause a diversion so someone else could move in?" I looked in the mirror nervously and at the cars scattered around us.

"I didn't see anyone else trying to maneuver into position. Carlson and Braddock have us flanked for the rest of the trip home. Don't worry."

By the time we rode into King George County and parked in front of the sheriff's office, I was just ready to be out of the car and indoors somewhere safe. Jack was taking too many chances being out like he was, and if these killers were as professional as everyone said they were, then two FBI agents and a mortician weren't going to be enough to stop them if they really wanted to get to Jack.

We made it inside and all of the cops that were on duty stopped what they were doing and stared. A few called out hellos and then everyone went back to whatever it is they were doing. There weren't a lot of high profile crimes that happened in this area, unless you counted the last six months or so where we had a serial killer and a shutdown of the largest hate crime organization in the state.

But there were other matters that kept Jack's cops busy, and he was understaffed, which was one of his frustrations with the political side of things. This was a high drug traffic area, especially for meth, since there was so much wooded land that could hide cooking labs easily. The good news was Jack didn't have to worry about funding for equipment and weapons. Every time they made a drug bust the money funded the sheriff's department.

Virginia also had the distinction of having some of the highest income areas in the nation dispersed amongst some of the lowest. They dealt with a lot of domestic disputes from both ends of the spectrum, as well as burglaries and car theft. The men who worked under Jack never had idle hands.

We turned toward Jack's office and I could see Agent Greer, Lauren Rhodes, and several other agents, along with boards similar to the ones we were using at home to lay out the crime scenes and any pertinent information.

Jack's office was a three-sided square of windows on the far side of the room. There were blinds available if he needed privacy for some reason, but he almost always had them open so his men knew they were welcome to stop in and run some-thing by him if they needed to. His desk was metal and dented in the front and the carpet was threadbare. There were two visitors' chairs, file cabinets made of the same metal as his desk, and a plant that had seen better days on top of the file cabinet. It was stark and meant as a place to work, and his men respected him more for it.

"They're making themselves right at home, aren't they?" I said.

"I gave them permission to use it as a home base, but I'm not going to let the feds knock me off my turf and take over completely. Greer's pissed that Carver has come in to help me, and this is his way of poking back a little."

"Speaking of Carver, where is he?"

"He's taking care of re-interviewing friends and family of those involved in the heist. We'll see if he can find any connections that were missed before. Carver's been working on this new computer program. I told you he was a genius, right?"

"You mentioned it. And he likes to mention it to me whenever you're not in the room while he gives me the spiel about how he and I should ditch you and his wife and take off for the tropics. He's under the impression the impressiveness of his brains will sway me."

"What'd you tell him?"

"I told him I was shallow and more impressed by—" I looked down below his belt and then back up at Jack in time to catch his smile. "The size of a man's ego."

His grin spread and he tossed an arm around my shoulders, pulling me close. "That's harsh. But funny."

"Carver's got a weird sense of humor. He said he knew first hand he'd lose that battle every time and that I'm supposed to ask you about the Sophia Landon case the two of you worked together."

I wasn't sure I'd ever seen Jack blush before, but his cheeks turned ruddy even as his grin went a bit sheepish. "Never in a million years. Maybe I need to have a little talk with Carver."

Detective Colburn intercepted us before we made it to Jack's office. "I didn't know you'd appointed the feds to take over while you were on vacation. I thought Lewis's eyes were going to bug out of his head when one of the agents leaned over his shoulder this morning and started reading a report he was typing up."

Jack's eyes narrowed and he nodded. "I'll take care of it."

"They're letting me sit in on the investigation. Giving me busy work for the most part, but I don't mind. I want to see it through. The vic was mine."

"Then let's go see what they have to say."

No one really paid attention when we went in the office. One of the other agents had made himself comfortable behind Jack's desk, the coffee mug I'd given Jack for Christmas one year, sitting at his elbow.

Jack pulled Greer aside, giving him no choice but to talk with him over in the corner. I could see Jack's face. It was calm as he explained something in great detail, but Greer's shoulders stiffened and his fingers tapped against his thigh. Jack might have hated politics, but he was a natural at it. He was good at keeping the peace and negotiating to get exactly what he wanted. I had a feeling Greer had just been expertly negotiated.

Greer nodded and the two men shook hands before Jack went to the center of the room to look at the updated boards. I decided it was probably a good time to head to the coffee pot, and took one of the little Styrofoam cups someone had set out.

Lauren Rhodes had been on her phone on the opposite side of the room. As soon as she hung up, she focused in on Jack and started in his direction. I wasn't about to be left out, so I moved in and stood just behind her. She didn't notice me there, but Jack did and he shook his head a little in warning.

"I heard about the tail." She laid her hand on Jack's shoulder and it was everything I could do not to bare my teeth. "You need to be more careful. Even with the added protection you don't need to be going out unnecessarily, and surely you don't need to endanger a civilian by letting her tag along."

I assumed the civilian she was speaking of was me, and I took a fortifying sip of coffee so my mouth would be full and I wouldn't say anything.

"I don't want to see anything happen to you, Jack. You need to lay low for a while until this blows over. Maybe take a trip to the beach house for a few weeks."

"Yeah, Jack," I said, widening my eyes dramatically and batting my eyelashes. "Maybe Lauren's right. You don't want to take any unnecessary chances. And a trip to the beach house sounds nice."

Lauren turned in surprise and almost bumped my coffee cup, and I saw Jack roll his eyes while her back was turned and mouth the words *behave yourself.*

No way in hell, I mouthed as soon as Lauren turned back to Jack. And dammit, her hand went right to his arm again. I narrowed my eyes and looked between where she was touching and the annoyance on Jack's face, and nodded in approval when he took a step back out of her reach.

"Lauren, no offense to the agents who are covering my tail because I'm damned glad for the extra eyes, but I've been Special Forces, been through training at Quantico with several of the agents in this room, and I spent ten years on SWAT. Believe me when I tell you I'm more than qualified to handle myself in a situation, and I'm trained to watch for threats. And my safety isn't what's at stake here. It's finding whoever the hell hunted and killed my men. I won't stop until I've found every one of them and made sure they've paid."

Lauren nodded and took a step back. "I told my boss that's more than likely what you'd say."

"I'd sure like to know what kind of interest your boss has in this case."

Lauren's lips twitched. "We all have a job to do."

Agent Greer chose that moment to get everyone's attention. "Let's get this briefing started. I want you to remember that Sheriff Lawson has volunteered his office as well as the use of the storage room to the back. We appreciate the hospitality, Sheriff. And my agents will remember that the cops out front all have jobs to do and aren't their gophers nor do they need help doing their jobs."

The statement was made publicly, and there were a few uncomfortable looks from a couple of the agents.

"The faster we can find these bastards the faster we can be out of your hair."

Jack nodded in thanks. "If you need a couple of extra hands

I've earmarked Detectives Colburn and Lewis. I'm sure we can all work together on this. What did you find?"

"Organized killing of this kind and with the skill they used isn't done by amateurs," Greer said. "These were hired hits. It's not going to be mob related. They can't agree on what kind of guns to use, much less how to kill nine highly trained men. So that leaves us with the gangs. Specifically the Vagos."

"We've gotten word the Vagos have seen a heavy increase in their cash flow the last few months. A motorcycle gang based out of California, they now have organized factions in fourteen different states. A large percentage of members are former military, either dishonorably discharged or disenfranchised with the military or the government in general, so they're highly trained and skilled. Their main targets are law enforcement, so if they were offered a price per head for specific law enforcement targets, then it's a job they likely wouldn't refuse. There's not a crime the Vagos haven't committed, and they're highly dangerous and on the top of our watch list. Catching them isn't going to be easy."

"We've got to follow the money," Jack said, looking at the board and the pictures of several gang members who had the military training to pull the job off. "We've got motive. This is a revenge killing, plain and simple. And we have the means since whoever has orchestrated this is using the Vagos Gang as their personal killing machine. But we've got to find the money and cut off the funds."

"Exactly," Greer said. "Every agent and officer in this room has a list of people involved and their financials. We're going to dig and dig deeper until we find something that connects somehow. How did your meeting with Jane Elliott go?"

Jack shrugged. "About as well as could be expected. She's confused and hurt and angry. I told her to call me if she remembered anything, no matter how small, but I have a feeling she won't. She doesn't want to think about what happened six years ago. Her life was hell then."

"We're going to head out and meet up with Carver. We'll keep you updated on our end of things."

"I need to get some work done at the funeral home," I piped in. "I've got a viewing scheduled for the end of the week, but I need to make all the necessary arrangements. It shouldn't take me more than a half hour though. If you need to meet with Carver we can split up for an hour."

Jack was already shaking his head. "We stick together. There's safety in numbers. I've got patrolmen out scoping the perimeters, and it's going to be damned hard for anyone to get close enough to take me out in a crowd. We'll go tend to your body. Leanne deserves whatever time you can give to her."

I nodded and wished I could feel as confident about the whole situation as Jack did. I didn't have a good feeling in the pit of my stomach, but in all fairness, I hadn't really had a good feeling in my stomach since I'd been almost strangled to death by someone I'd known almost my whole life. I just hoped it was a residual effect and wasn't my intuition finally coming out to play.

14

AGENT BRADDOCK FOLLOWED US TO THE FRONT OF THE station. My arms were full with files and the financial information Jack and Carver would be sifting through later. Jack and Braddock needed to keep their hands free, so I'd been chosen as pack mule until we got back to the car.

The sun glared brightly as we walked outside, and I realized it was the first time I'd seen it in several days. The weather had been bleary and bleak, with nothing but heavy clouds and rain for more than a week. I was hoping the sun would dry out the ground some. My workers had a grave to dig for Leanne Mosely and it would be horrible messy work if it stayed as wet as it had been.

I'd left my sunglasses at home and squinted as we made our way down the bricked sidewalk toward the parking lot.

"Don't," Jack said, and when I looked up I realized he was talking to Braddock. "Keep moving."

It was then I noticed the man across the street. He headed toward us, his hands in his pockets and his head down. He wore a light grey jacket and had the hood pulled up over his head. He moved quickly and with purpose, and when he looked up his eyes were trained on Jack. He looked down again just as quickly.

"Jaye, get in the driver's seat. Braddock, you're going to need to stay back and not interfere. Just follow behind us like normal. I've got this covered."

Jack pulled out his gun and checked the magazine and got into the back seat of the Jeep. Braddock didn't look happy, but Jack closed the door in his face and he had no choice but to move to the panel van parked a few cars back from us.

I wanted to ask questions, but I could feel Jack's urgency. I dumped the files in the back seat and then climbed in and turned over the engine.

"What's going on?"

"Unlock the doors and keep looking straight ahead. No matter what happens you keep driving, okay?"

Jack sat in the middle of the back seat and leaned forward, the gun held loosely in his hand. He gave my shoulder a quick squeeze and I unlocked the doors. When I pulled to the stoplight the passenger door opened, and I had to hold back a scream when the man in the gray jacket got in beside me.

Jack pointed the gun at the man's head before he had the door shut all the way. The light turned green and I kept driving. Just like Jack had asked.

The man lifted his hands slowly and then pushed back the hood so his face showed. Even out of my periphery I got a good look at him. He was big like Jack, maybe a couple of inches shorter, though it was hard to tell. His hair was shaved so close to the scalp I couldn't tell what color it was and his nose had been broken at some point in his life.

"Commander Lawson," the man said. "What the *fuck* is going on?"

"You tell me, Wolfe." Jack's voice was as steady as the gun in his hand. "Nine of my men dead in the last few months. Nine of your brothers."

"And you think I'm the one responsible?" His anger lashed out at Jack and my hands tightened on the wheel. "You'll pardon me for repeating myself, but what the fuck?"

"You've been missing for four days. Completely off the grid. Wallace's body washed up not far from here. I can count on one finger the number of people I trust right now. If you're innocent then I'll apologize later. If you're not, then it won't matter one way or the other. Now start explaining."

"I felt eyes on me," Wolfe finally said. "For a couple of weeks now. I couldn't shake the feeling, but no matter how hard I looked or tried to trap them into slipping up I couldn't see who was watching. I knew I was either going crazy or bad shit was going down.

"I actually called Wallace the day before I went off the grid. He'd felt the eyes on him as well, and we agreed to meet. Wallace was always better at keeping up with everyone than I was, and he told me the others had been taken out. That it looked like we were all being ambushed and eliminated. He didn't know who or why, but I could tell he was shaken. And you know nothing ever shook Wallace. He said we'd make contact with you and then maybe disappear for a little while until we could get it figured out."

"How'd you find out about Wallace?"

"He missed the meet. Five A.M. Lexington Street Bridge. He was going to boost a car and we'd do a quick grab and switch when he picked me up. I packed weapons and other essentials in my pack and then set out to meet him. I knew when he didn't make the drive by that something was wrong. Wallace never flaked on a mission. I didn't hang around, afraid if they'd somehow gotten Wallace to talk that there would be men waiting for me too. I switched plates and boosted a car of my own, but I had to make sure about Wallace. I set up shop on the roof of a house across the street from his. It was still dark out so I was hidden. I used my scope to look through Wallace's windows. I could see the place was torn to shit, so I packed up, boosted another car and came looking for you.

"I didn't know you had federal protection until they tried to corner me today on your drive back from Fairfax."

"That was you?" I asked incredulously. "You scared the hell out of me."

"If you don't mind me pointing out the obvious, you don't look so calm right now either. And you just ran that stop sign."

"I'm going to kill your friend, Jack."

"Oddly enough, you're not the first woman I've heard say that." Jack's weapon was still trained on Wolfe. "I'm going to trust you because my gut is telling me I don't really have a choice. But if you turn out to be responsible for even a tiny sliver of this, I promise there won't be a hole you can hide in where I won't find you."

"Ditto, Commander. I'm just as pissed off as you are."

"Maybe the two of you should seal it over a beer and by swinging your dicks around."

"She's kind of feisty, Jack. I like that in a woman. Are you single, sugar?"

"Mother of God," I said, turning onto Catherine of Aragon. "You must hang out with Carver."

"Carver's here?" Wolfe asked, rubbing his hands together. "Excellent."

"Wolfe, this is Doctor J.J. Graves. She's very good with a scalpel, just as a fair warning."

"Is she yours?"

"Every feisty inch of her."

"You always did have all the luck."

"You're both crazy." I pulled into the driveway of the funeral home and under the portico, and Agent Braddock was right behind us. "I've got some work to do." I started to open the door but Jack stopped me.

"Wait a second, Jaye. Let Wolfe get out first. Braddock will cover him while we get out of the car."

"If I didn't understand your worry, I'd be really pissed off about you treating me like a criminal."

"I guess it's a good thing you understand then," Jack said.

I waited as Wolfe got out of the car slowly, showing his hands to Agent Braddock as the agent kept a close eye on him. I got out of the car and Jack kept his weapon out, searching the area.

"Just leave the files in the car," he said. "We'll give them to Carver once we get back to the house."

Jack went inside first, followed by me and Wolfe, and then Braddock taking up the rear. They did a quick walkthrough of the funeral home, even Wolfe, who had his own weapon in his hands as he opened closet doors with quick efficiency.

I started a pot of coffee and let them do their thing, but when Wolfe came back into the kitchen without Jack or Braddock, I couldn't seem to take my eyes off the dull sheen of the gun in his hands. So long as I lived and breathed I could have gone without looking down the barrel of a loaded weapon again.

"I see you can't take your eyes off it," Wolfe said. "I've got to admit it's pretty impressive. Bigger than Jack's even." His lips twitched with good humor and he stood still, letting me get used to him.

My gaze went to his face and I watched him carefully, making no apologies for my thorough study. His eyes were a light brown and I recognized them as belonging to a cop. I remembered that Wolfe had turned in his badge and become a P.I, so he wasn't a cop any longer, but that didn't make the look go away. He was built like a fighter and held his weapon with ease.

"You want some coffee?" I asked.

"I wouldn't turn it down. So you and Jack, huh? He used to keep a picture of you and a couple of other guys on his desk. You were all covered in mud and he had his arm slung around you. Both of you grinning like fools."

I smiled as I poured his coffee and handed it to him. "Flag football. We won."

Wolfe took a sip of coffee and grimaced. "Jesus. This is terrible coffee. It's just like being back at the cop shop."

"Jack normally makes it. I've got milk if you think that will help."

"No need. My stomach lining is already half gone."

Jack came in at that moment and smirked when he saw Wolfe was drinking coffee. "You always had more bravery than brains." He grabbed a water from the fridge and took the barstool across from Wolfe. "Despite the circumstance, it's good to see you again. I asked Braddock to give us some time so I could catch you up on things. You'll stay in one of the guest rooms at our house until this is resolved."

"I'd appreciate it. And remember, I've made a hell of a lot of contacts in my line of work over the past several years. I can use them if you need me to."

"I appreciate the offer."

"I'll be in my office," I said, refilling my cup and heading out the door. "I'll be ready in about half an hour."

Five minutes after the time I'd told them I made my way back into the kitchen. I'd scheduled flowers, catering, my gravediggers, and made sure I had the casket Mark Mosely had ordered in stock. I'd also contacted the paper and sent them the obituary. The viewing would be Friday night and the funeral early Saturday morning. It would be a packed house.

"You all set?" Jack asked.

"I'm good. Did he catch you up on everything we have so far?" I asked Wolfe.

"He did. And I'm looking forward to seeing the boards you have set up. I'm a champion at research. Have to be in my line of work. I'm ready to take these bastards out."

"You and me both," I said.

Jack grinned and pulled me close, kissing me on the temple. "Can't wait to get me to the altar, can you?"

Wolfe whistled long and low. "She must be some kind of voodoo woman to have talked you into that. I didn't think Lawson would ever take the plunge."

I elbowed Jack in the gut before he could say anything inappropriate, and both men chuckled. Braddock came into the kitchen, and his serious demeanor put a damper on things.

I was used to working with cops. There was a certain rhythm between us all as we worked a scene, but even at the worst scenes cops had a sense of humor. It was the same way with morticians. The humor leaned toward the macabre and would probably be seen as inappropriate to outsiders. It was either learn to have a sense of humor or break down into tears. Every cop I know would say it was better to laugh than to cry. Once you started crying it was sometimes hard to stop.

Braddock opened the kitchen door to lead us out, his weapon down at his side, and this time Wolfe and I were in the middle and Jack brought up the rear. Braddock made it to the bottom of the steps when he staggered backward, and then the report of a rifle echoed in my ears.

Braddock fell on top of Wolfe, causing a domino effect, and for that reason alone the shot that hit Wolfe didn't hit dead in the center of his chest. I fell backwards, the weight of Wolfe and Braddock pinning me down. My back hit the doorknob and my head rapped against the edge of the counter. Jack was still inside, and I thanked God for small favors. Another bullet shattered the glass in the kitchen door and I felt the sting of cuts as glass rained down on top of us.

"Pull them in," I yelled over the rushing in my ears. I had Wolfe in a hold under his armpits and I dragged him back into the kitchen while Jack did the same with Braddock. It had been a long time since I'd been in an emergency room type situation, but the flow came back as I quickly assessed the damage to Wolfe.

Jack slammed the kitchen door closed and bolted it and then knelt down beside Braddock. The bullet had hit Wolfe high in the shoulder. It wasn't a life-threatening wound, but he was losing blood. He was conscious and looked more pissed off than hurt.

"Jack, go down to the lab and grab my big medical bag. The one I keep under the counter."

He did as I asked and disappeared through the metal door that led down to the lab. We'd positioned both bodies behind the island for a little protection in case the windows were shot out, but it wouldn't be much. I reached into the drawer without standing up and felt around for a couple of cup towels.

"You're going to have to apply the pressure. I need to get to Braddock." I slapped a towel on his back where the bullet had exited and another on top at the entry wound, and then I crawled across the floor to see to Braddock.

He wasn't in good shape. I heard the faint whistling sound

from his chest telling me his lung had collapsed and pink foam bubbled at the corners of his blue-tinged lips. He was conscious, his eyes wheeling around and his pupils the size of pinpricks.

Jack's footsteps echoed off the stairs as he ran back up, and he knelt by my side with my bag.

"Do you need help with this? The sooner I can call it in the better."

"I've got it. Go ahead." I'd already dismissed him in my mind. I was completely focused on Braddock and I knew we were playing against the clock. He wasn't bleeding from underneath, so I knew the bullet was still lodged inside him somewhere.

I didn't have time to put on surgical gloves. I just had to stop the air that was leaking from that lung. I cut away his shirt. I didn't have any one-way valves in my supplies. I wasn't equipped to work on the living. So I cut off the fingertip of a surgical glove and inserted a 14-gauge needle. He needed something that would stop the air from escaping and a valve, even homemade, would stop the leak and reinflate the lung.

I carefully inserted the needle between the second and third intercostal space at the mid clavicular line, and there was a sudden gush of air as Braddock was able to draw in a breath. He was still losing a lot of blood, and I had a feeling the bullet had hit something else of importance, but there wasn't much more I could do without a hospital and the proper equipment.

I heard sirens in the distance and Jack was keeping his hand pressed to the compresses on Wolfe's shoulder.

"Change them out," I told him. "In the drawer above your head."

He nodded and made the switch quickly, tossing the bloodied rags aside. I could see the anger on Jack's face. Some of the flying glass had cut his cheek and neck and blood dripped down onto the collar of his shirt.

He got on the phone again and whoever picked up got the full force of his anger. "I want answers and I want them now," he said. "This town is crawling with FBI agents and you can't find someone that's carrying around a sniper rifle and shooting people?"

Jack was quiet for a minute and then his jaw clenched. "I've got officers responding and the paramedics are on the way. And we're going to have a long conversation the next time we see each other."

The responding officers identified themselves as they neared the house, and Jack got up to let them in. He still had his weapon in his hand, and I saw when Martinez and Chen came inside they had theirs out as well.

"They've got the area cordoned off and we've got officers patrolling in the area you thought the shots came from," Martinez said. "We're stepping on some federal toes, and they're not too happy about it."

"You have no idea how sad that makes me," Jack said. "How far behind are the paramedics?"

"About another minute."

"You and Chen are going to personally accompany Wolfe to the hospital," Jack said, pointing to his friend. "You're going to stay with him through treatment and then accompany him back to my house. He's not to have any visitors other than the medical personnel, and you stay with him round the clock."

"Yes, sir," Martinez nodded.

"What about the other one?" Chen asked.

"He wasn't the target. He just happened to be first in line. If Greer feels he needs added protection he can assign some, but I don't think it's necessary."

A crackle of sound came through on the radio on Chen and Martinez's duty belts. "This is Lewis. I've got a possible shooter site. I'm not seeing any empty cartridges, but the location is right and the ground is disturbed. I've got a team coming in to see if we can find anything useful."

Martinez handed Jack the microphone attached to his collar so he could answer. "Good work Lewis. Have Sergeant Smith reassign all active cases to Cole and Durrant. I want everyone else split up into teams and working the area in grids. Have him organize it quickly. It's taking the FBI too fucking long to get their shit together. And I can't decide if they're really here for the reasons they say they are, or if they have another agenda."

"You got it, boss."

Chen went over to let the paramedics inside. I kept my fingers on the pulse at Braddock's wrist. He'd lost consciousness, but he was still breathing, though those breaths were getting shallower by the minute.

"Good to see you, Doctor Graves," one of the paramedics said. I recognized him from when I'd worked at the hospital. He had a lot of years in and good hands. He knelt down across from me.

"Percy," I acknowledged. "Gunshot wound to the chest. Collapsed lung. Bullet's still in there."

Percy placed an endotracheal tube down his throat. "Good thing you were here. He wouldn't have had a chance without a doctor close by."

I moved out of the way so Percy's partner could start an IV, and another two paramedics moved in to treat Wolfe.

"I'm fine," Wolfe said. "It's a through and through. Just sew me back up and give me some fluids."

"I see you're an expert at this," one of the paramedics said. "But it looks like a surgeon is going to have to see you. It looks like you've got fibers inside and you could have some damage."

Wolfe gave Jack a narrowed look, and I could see Jack wanted to smile. "Be good and go with them."

"I don't want to miss out on the takedown. I'm not staying the night."

"Fine. As long as you don't fall down from blood loss, you're in."

"Let's get moving then," Wolfe grouched. They strapped Wolfe to a board and lifted him to the gurney, and they were rolling out the kitchen door. Jack nodded to Martinez and Chen and they followed him out.

It was only a few more minutes until they had Braddock stable enough to move. Jack and I were in the wreckage of the kitchen alone. I heard the other cops outside of the funeral home, but the adrenaline was starting to catch up with me. I needed to stay busy.

Jack's phone rang. "It's Carver," he said, looking at the screen. He answered and I went to the drawer for some more clean towels and then wetted them. Jack switched the phone to his other ear so I could wipe away the blood on the right side of his face and see how bad the cuts were.

"I want you to start digging, Carver," he said, hissing as the water touched one of the deeper cuts. "Find out why the DOJ is involved. Their interest in this isn't because of me or what happened six years ago. Greer and Lauren are holding some-thing back."

Thankfully none of the cuts on his face or neck needed stitches, and for the most part they'd already stopped bleed-ing, with the exception of a couple that had already turned sluggish.

"Yeah, we're fine," he said to Carver. "Just scratches. We'll be back to the house soon."

Jack disconnected, took the towel from my hand, and tossed it in the sink. He wet the other towel I'd laid on the counter and then took my face in his hands gently as he doctored the cuts on my face and neck. I'd realized when the glass shat-tered that I'd caught a few stray cuts, but I'd stopped feeling them the moment I'd focused on Wolfe and Braddock.

"Not too bad," he said, kissing me on the forehead. "You're okay."

"Just another day at the office."

He laughed and buried his face against my hair. "It's starting to seem that way, isn't it? I'd give anything for you to not be in harm's way, but I'm glad you were here today. Braddock is alive because of it and probably Wolfe too."

"I guess getting shot was a good way to prove he's not involved."

"It lessens the chances. I'm going to have a couple of officers follow us back to the house. Once we get back I'll call and have a cleaning crew come take care of the mess here and replace the window in the door."

"Sounds good," I nodded. "Let's go home. I could use a glass of wine or three."

15

JACK HAD JUST TURNED ONTO HERESY ROAD WHEN MY CELL phone rang. I looked at the caller ID, but the number was blocked. When I showed it to Jack he got out his own phone and started dialing.

"Go ahead and answer it. Maybe we can get a trace on it."

"Doctor Graves," I said, answering the call.

"Jack has some bad enemies." It was my father. I knew it would be. "Tell him I caught a glimpse of a man named Jesse Tydell over in King George Proper. He's a captain for the Vagos motorcycle gang. Lots of kills under his belt. Ex-military with an expert marksman rating. He won't be here alone. You and Jack got lucky today. Maybe you need to disappear for a little while."

"Dad—" It's all I got to say before he disconnected. "Dammit." I tossed the phone into my bag.

"Not enough time," he said, disconnecting. "Maybe Carver

can work some magic on your phone when we get back. What did your dad say?"

"That you need to be looking for a man named Jesse Tydell. He's a captain for the Vagos. Dad saw him over in King George and he says he's ex-military and an expert marksman."

Jack got back on the phone and relayed the information to someone—I was guessing Greer.

"Your dad seems to have a lot of knowledge about this."

"I think he's worried about me. About you too."

And the knowledge was playing havoc with my emotions. I'd spent the last two years building up my hatred for my parents, convincing myself that I'd have been better to never know them at all. That they were nothing more than liars and thieves, and probably killers. It had festered inside of me—the hatred—and it gave me something to hold on to as guilt and blame weighed down on my own shoulders.

I'd wondered more than once if I should have known or realized something was going on. It happened right under my nose. And a small part of me wondered if what the police had said was really true—that my parents had been having problems and driven over that cliff on purpose. I'd been ashamed almost more over that than the illegal activities, which made no sense at all. But them committing double suicide had shaken the very foundation of my world—my upbringing.

My parents had been a lot of things during my childhood— they'd worked too much, missing softball games and the occasional school play—but they'd provided me with security, an education, and I never went hungry. They didn't provide love, but maybe it just wasn't in them to do so. And it worried me that being unable to love was something I might suffer from when I had children of my own.

"He told us we need to get out of town. Lay low for awhile."

"I'm starting to think maybe that's not such a bad idea. At least for you."

"I'm going to pretend you didn't just say that." The squad car behind us stayed close and I saw another parked along the road next to the turn in to Jack's house.

"Don't be stubborn about this, Jaye."

"Do you see this big ass ring that's sitting on my finger? It means that my place is with you. Period. You're not going to send me away so you can be shot at all alone. If that's what you're aiming for, then I'm more than of shooting at you."

Jack snorted out a laugh. "I'm sure you would."

He did a u-turn in the driveway and then backed into the garage so he was facing out. The garage was attached to the house and there was an entry door into the mudroom. He closed the garage door and we went inside.

Carver was in the kitchen making a sandwich. He was still FBI pressed and polished, but his hair was disheveled as if he'd been running his fingers through it over and over again.

"Oh, good. You're back," he said. "And alive. A team is being put together to check out the tip about Jesse Tydell and any known associates. If he's here, we'll run him to ground. How do the two of you feel about a trip to D.C.?"

"It depends. Are you trying to put us in a safe house?" Jack asked.

Carver's lips twitched before he took a giant bite of sand-wich. "I would if I didn't know you'd cut my balls off with that knife you carry in your boot. But no, that's not my objective."

"I'm listening."

"Eric and Karl Lieber's parents are stateside. They were staying at their home in New York and we were able to subpoena them to come to D.C. to be reinterviewed. I thought you might like to be there."

"Greer's letting you take that?"

"Oh, yeah. We're a team. Don't you know the FBI motto?" The look on Carver's face insinuated they were anything but. "But I actually agree with Greer on this one. It'll help to get the two of you out of here while they're running Jesse Tydell to ground. We don't want him to get another shot at you."

"I'd prefer him not get another shot at me either. I'm just surprised Greer is agreeing to let you take point with this."

"Greer and I have come to an understanding. I'm here because you're my friend and you asked me to be here. Though I'm pretty sure you didn't ask me to come for this. Maybe we'll get to that at some point, hmm?" He looked at me and I smiled innocently. I wasn't sure I was ready to let anyone besides Jack see those boxes. "This isn't my case. It's Greer's. And though I could take it from him if I wanted to, I don't really want to. He's doing a thorough job and he's good at what he does. He's not the one you have to worry about."

"Lauren," Jack said, nodding. "I had a feeling she was up to something."

"She's up to wanting you back. That much is obvious."

"He's not available," I said. I grabbed a soda from the fridge instead of getting another cup of coffee.

"Do you think there's a chance you and Lauren will get into a fight?" Carver asked. "Maybe pull some hair. And maybe Lauren rips your blouse some and while you're both rolling around in the mud her skirt could ride up around her waist."

"I guess you've put some thought into that scenario," I said.

"Only before I go to bed every night."

"Oh, good. That makes it less creepy."

"You sound like my wife." The look on his face was so forlorn I had to laugh.

"I'd like to meet your wife some time."

"You'd probably like each other a lot. She's always threatening to kill me."

"I know a lot of different ways to kill a person. Maybe I can give her some tips."

He gave a long, low whistle and looked at Jack. "And you're going to marry this woman? She's pretty scary."

Jack grinned and winked at me. "I like to live on the edge. Now tell me what you found out about the DOJ."

"Word has it they knew from the start that the Vagos were involved in this. The Department of Justice has been trying to get a leg up on them for almost a decade. They haven't been able to penetrate and it's one of the largest gangs where they don't have someone on the inside. Lauren's here to make sure the Vagos who were hired stay alive. She's hoping she can get one to turn and give inside information."

Jack's arms crossed over his chest and his face went to stone. "She wants them to walk after they killed my men? Nine men and an attempt on Wolfe and she just wants them to go free in exchange for information."

Carver wisely stayed silent and watched Jack over his sandwich. I was really starting to dislike Lauren.

"Fuck that, Carver. If I get the opportunity I'm taking them out. Where does Greer stand on this?"

"I'm not sure he really knows why she's here because it was need to know information and Greer doesn't have the clearance. I don't either, but I've got my ways." Carver sighed and dropped the rest of his sandwich on his plate, pushing it away.

"Listen, Jack. I can't say that I wouldn't do the same thing if I were in your shoes. I'm staying neutral in this. But you don't want to cross the DOJ if you can help it. Lauren might want you in her bed, but she'll slit your throat if it will further her career."

"I'll handle Lauren. Thanks for finding out the information."

"I'm adding it to your tab. You owe me just over a billion dollars, but I'll call it a clean slate if you babysit for me and Michelle and let us get away for a weekend. Do you know how long it's been since I've slept an entire night?"

"That's what you get for being so virile," Jack said. "It's the price you pay for your manhood."

"I guess when you put it that way I am a pretty impressive specimen." He buffed his fingers on the front of his shirt.

"You want a sandwich before we leave for D.C?" Jack asked me, taking the stuff from Carver and making one for himself.

"No, I'm not hungry. And I've still got blood under my fingernails and on my clothes. I'm going to shower and change."

"You sure do take a lot of showers."

"Death is a messy business. Is this an overnight trip or are we coming back tonight?"

"Pack a bag," Carver said. "We'll come back first thing in the morning. It'll give the guys a little longer to look for Jesse and his friends."

———

An hour later Jack and I were both showered and changed and we were headed to D.C. in Carver's government issue SUV.

"I started combing all of the financials that came in," Carver said. "You told me that Katie Elliott's experimental cancer treatment was paid for by an organization called Kids With Cancer. From what I can tell it seems to be a huge non-profit organization and all legit on the surface. The money goes to the kids."

"What about underneath the surface?" Jack asked.

"That's always the kicker. About six months before the Federal Reserve heist a two million dollar donation was given to Kids With Cancer anonymously. That was the largest single donation by one patron they'd had since the charity's inception."

"Can you see who the anonymous donor was?"

"It's going to take some digging with my lady love."

Carver was referring to his computer. He seemed to have unnatural feelings for an object that plugged into the wall. Of course, before I'd met Jack and was having regular sex I'd had unnatural feelings for an object that had plugged into the wall too.

"They've got the money hidden behind a bunch of bogus corporations. But if we keep following the money we'll get to the right spot."

"Did you find anything else in the financials?" Jack asked.

"That wasn't enough? You're going to be babysitting for a whole week if you don't start showing some appreciation."

"Fine. I'll start digging through the research and you walk around town dressed like me to see if one of the Vagos will shoot you in the street."

"When you put it that way I should probably stick with the research. My wife hates it when I get shot."

"I can sympathize," I said. "I've never been very fond of Jack getting shot either. Are you sure no one is following us?"

"We're in the clear. We loaded you up in the garage and you hid in the back. As far as anyone watching the house is concerned we were just changing shifts. And we've got two federal cars following us now just to make sure."

"Did you check out Wolfe?" Jack asked. "Any money problems?"

"I know everything about him down to what kind of underwear he likes to buy. He's clean so far as I can tell. His business is good. He's a solid P.I. with a good staff, and this is D.C. so you know there are plenty of people always spying on other people. Wolfe makes more than you and I put together and then some. He's not having money problems at all.

"He does, however, seem to have women problems. He goes through them like Kleenex. The girl he's seeing now—the one who reported him missing—her name's Lisa. They've been together a couple of weeks. She wasn't very helpful when questioned. She didn't even know what his last name was or what he did for a living. According to her he looked like the ultimate bad boy and the tats on his chest are smokin'." He paused for a second. "I guess that's a good thing?"

"Oh, it's definitely a good thing," I said, thinking of Jack's tattoo. It never failed to drive me crazy. Jack looked at me and raised a brow and I could tell he knew exactly what I was thinking.

"Knock it off. You're fogging up my windows." Carver flipped on the wipers as a light drizzle started to fall. "So much for the sunny weather. Stupid springtime."

Carver maneuvered through D.C. traffic at top speed and I sat back and buckled my seatbelt as the rain started falling a little harder.

"Anyway, I combed through the files on all of your men. They were mostly in good shape. A couple had some debt trouble, but nothing severe. I didn't see any evidence that anyone besides Elliott was on the take or involved with the heist. And I looked damned close."

"What about family members of the robbers?"

"I'm still wading through that. Greer divided up the financials between his men to go through, but I told them to just send it all to me. I've got a computer program that can do it faster. We should have more information by the time we get back to Bloody Mary tomorrow. What the hell kind of name is that for a town anyway? Creeps me out."

Carver drove into the parking garage at the J. Edgar Hoover Building. I've never been a fan of parking garages. First of all, they were confusing and I could never figure out how to get out. Second of all, they were dark and seemed like a really good place to kill someone. My only consolation was that I was with two armed men. I'd had to leave my gun in the car.

Once we got through security, Carver led us through a long hallway with gray industrial carpet that opened up into a large office space shared by several agents. The noise level was higher than I expected it to be. We turned off into a side hallway and Carver opened a door for us.

"You two watch in observation. If something they say clicks or you need me to follow up on something, just send a text." With that Carver shut the door and left Jack and I in a dark little room no bigger than the size of a large closet.

A man and woman sat at a table in the room next to ours, and I saw the door open as Carver stepped through and took a seat across from them. Jack adjusted the volume on the wall console.

"Thank you for being here, Mr. and Mrs. Lieber," Carver said. "We'll get this finished as quickly as possible."

"This is an outrage," the man said. His accent was prim and upper crust and his posture defensive with his arms crossed over his chest. His hair was solid silver and his face had bones of good breeding, much like his wife who sat next to him, her hands clutching a handbag worth more than I made in a month.

"We've sat through your interrogations before, and I don't see why we have to suffer through it again. Our children are dead. What more could you possibly try to take from us?"

"Harold, remember your blood pressure," the woman said, patting his hand gently. Her face was ashen but her eyes glittered with anger as she skewered Agent Carver with a look. "This is unconscionable. Haven't we suffered enough? We haven't been able to show our faces in our social circle for six years."

"It must be terrible," Carver said deadpan. "Mr. Lieber. You asked what more we could possibly take from you. Do you blame us for the death of your children? Despite the circumstances surrounding how they were killed?"

"You gunned them down like animals. They had brilliant minds. Both of them. Eric was a Rhodes scholar. And Karl had won more awards by the time he was twenty for the advancement of technology than most people will get in a lifetime. The medical examiner said Karl and Eric had a combined twenty-two gunshots to their bodies. I know how the police work. It's violence first. You thirst for it and bathe in the blood of your enemies."

Carver's brows arched. "You have a creative way with words. You forgot to mention the part where your sons killed almost twenty people, including a pregnant woman who was three weeks away from giving birth. Not to mention the fact that they broke into federal property, armed, and planned to steal millions of dollars. They also fired on the SWAT team that came in to neutralize them."

"It's in the past, Agent Carver. We'd like to get on with our lives." Harold Lieber scooted his chair back and moved to stand.

"Sit down, Mr. Lieber. We're not finished. You listed in your original statement that your sons' closest friends were Jordan Parker and Peter Anderson. They all grew up together, despite Peter being from London."

"They all attended the same boarding school together," Mrs. Lieber said, her composure slipping for the first time and the grief of a mother showing through. "The other boys, Jordan and Peter, would sometimes spend holidays at our house or our boys would spend time at theirs. They were all very close. We don't see the Andersons or the Parkers anymore. It's too painful for all of us."

"Were there other friends your boys spent as much time with as Jordan and Peter?"

"Just Paris Spencer," Mr. Lieber said. "She was like a kid sister to them all. She attended the same schools. She was devastated when they were killed."

"Was she romantically linked with any of them?"

"No, of course not. Why must you make things so sordid?"

"Just call me curious," Carver countered. He opened a thin file folder and pulled out a single sheet of paper. "Since your sons were killed it looks like your finances have suffered quite the setback."

"How dare you!" Lieber said, pushing back from the table. His chair hit the wall and toppled over onto its side. "How dare you look into our personal finances like we were nothing more than common criminals."

"It makes sense considering you raised common criminals."

Lieber's face turned an unhealthy shade of red. "Jesus," I said. "He's going to have a heart attack. I really don't want to have to give mouth to mouth to that man."

"He's got a hair trigger temper though. And a lot of pent up anger." Jack pulled me so I stood in front of him and then he wrapped his arms around my middle and rested his chin on the top of my head.

"Calm down, Harold," Mrs. Lieber said, patting him again, tears coursing down her cheeks. "Please."

"I only bring up your financials because you haven't adjusted your way of living and the debt is eating you alive. A new home, new cars, household staff. More than a hundred thousand dollars a year to something called WMF."

"It's a charitable organization," Mrs. Lieber said, sniffing delicately. "It stands for Wives and Mothers of the Fallen. I —" she paused and tried to compose herself, but she wasn't having much luck. "After the boys were killed they reached out to me. It's a support group as well. Widows and other mothers like me who have lost their children. And we raise money to help those who are like us and are struggling. It's a very worthy cause." She straightened her shoulders with dignity.

"What about you, Mr. Lieber? Any worthy causes you've been funding lately?"

"I don't have anything else to say to you. We're finished here." He held his hand out to his wife and helped her to stand.

"What if I told you the men who killed your sons in the line of duty were dead?"

"I'd say good riddance. It was no more than they deserved."

16

"DO YOU THINK HE'S RESPONSIBLE FOR THIS?" I ASKED A couple of hours later.

Carver had checked us all in to the hotel closest to the federal building, and I wondered if the bureau owned it considering the décor was very similar—meaning everything was industrial grade and the people behind the counters looked and acted like off duty cops. We'd dropped our luggage in the room and had come down to the restaurant to get some dinner. The food was mediocre at best, but at least my stomach wasn't rumbling anymore.

"I don't know," Jack said. "But he certainly has motive. And he has the temper. But I'm not sure he has the organizational and leadership skills it would take to plan a hit like this. The financial trouble is worrisome."

"Or maybe he's just putting everything he's got behind hiring out these hits. How much do you think he'd be paying the Vagos for that many kills?"

"Millions. And it would be a beneficial arrangement for both sides. Lieber gets his revenge and the Vagos pad their coffers to take over more territory."

"Have you told Carver anything about my dad?"

"About him being alive you mean? Because I'm pretty sure everyone in the FBI knows about your dad otherwise."

I rolled my eyes and tore off a hunk of bread. "Yes, I mean about him being alive."

"I told you I wouldn't until you were ready. A little trust would be nice, Doctor Graves."

"I know. I'm sorry." I sighed and tossed the bread to the plate, dusting off my hands. "This whole thing just has me twisted up in knots. Maybe we could give Carver a few of the flash drives without telling him where they came from. Without telling him my dad is alive."

"We could. But if he breaks through the encryption it probably won't take him long to figure out who they came from."

"He'll have to tell his superiors once he finds out."

"Yeah, he'll have to tell. And there will be questions. But it's nothing we can't handle together."

"Do you wonder if there ever will be? Anything we can't handle, I mean." I took a sip of wine and twisted the stem back and forth between my fingers. "Reverend Thomas always says that God won't give you more than you can handle. Do you think that's true? Because it feels like over the last year or so that He's really trying to test my limits."

"You never ask the easy questions." Jack took my wine from my hand and entwined his fingers with mine. "I don't want to disagree with Reverend Thomas, and if you ever tell him

I did I'll deny it, but it seems to me God doesn't have much to do with it. Don't get me wrong. I believe He's there and that there's something more after we die. But it seems to me that one of the biggest things He gave us is choice. Back to when Adam and Eve were in the garden, right? And people make choices, and their choices snowball and affect other people.

"Everything you've gone through this last year has been because another person made a bad choice. And I think because God gave people the ability to make those choices, He's not going to step in and interfere just because it may be more than you can handle. There are going to be times for both of us when it seems like it's more than we can deal with. I've been there. Back when I was looking down the barrel of a gun that belonged to a man I thought was my friend. Back when the pain from the bullets was so much that I was begging to die."

"Oddly enough, Jack, this pep talk isn't really all that comforting."

"What I'm saying is if I'd been alone, yeah, it would've been too much for me to handle. I'm not sure I'd ever have fully recovered. Maybe my body would have. But not my mind. But you were there. Even though things were different between us then than they are now. You were there. And you saved me."

I blinked the tears from my eyes and looked at him. Really looked at him. It never ceased to amaze me that he was mine. And I knew he was right. He was there. And he'd saved me too.

"You are going to get so lucky for that later," I grinned.

"What's this talk about later?" He charged the meal to our room and signed his name. "Now is as good a time as any."

"I guess when you put it that way." I laughed as I sprinted out of the restaurant and to the elevator. I punched the button and heard Jack yell, "Hey! Wait up!"

The doors slid open and Jack moved in behind me pushing me against the wall of the elevator. I couldn't have said at that moment if there were other people on there with us or how Jack managed to hit the right button for our floor. All I knew was his mouth was hot and open against mine and his body was pressed deliciously against the ache between my legs.

"This is probably illegal," I panted as his hand snaked beneath my shirt and palmed my breast. My eyes crossed as his thumb did something miraculous to my nipple.

"Good thing I have connections."

The elevator doors dinged open and Jack grasped me by the hips, his fingers branding me with their heat, and he walked down the long corridor to our room. At least I hoped it was our room.

"What about the surveillance cameras?" I bit at his bottom lip and sucked it into my mouth to soothe.

"I'll get Carver to erase them."

"Good thinking." My hand worked between our bodies, pulling at the button on his slacks and sliding inside to feel him hot and hard and ready. He sucked in a breath and stumbled at the touch and my back hit the door of our room.

I stroked him up and down while he swore and fumbled for the key. The door swung open at my back and we tumbled into the room, and Jack turned at the last minute so he landed on bottom and broke my fall. Blood rushed in my ears and I vaguely heard the door click shut behind us.

"This would be a lot easier if you wore skirts. I'd already be inside you." He tugged at my jeans and I pulled at the buttons on his shirt, sending them scattering in opposite directions.

"I'll remember that for next time." My jeans caught around my shoes and I kicked one off along with the pants leg. I heard a rip of material and felt my breath catch in my throat as he slid smoothly inside of me.

His muscles coiled and released as he began to move, and I felt myself helpless beneath the power of his touch. My legs tightened around him and my nails dug into his shoulders, looking for an anchor in the storm, and I cried out as I felt the first rolling wave shudder through my body.

His eyes met mine and I watched the dark brown bleed to black as he came closer and closer to his own fulfillment.

"I love you," he whispered against my lips. My hips arched into his and my breath hitched as another wave rocked through me, this one more powerful than the last, and I held on as he followed me into oblivion.

It took several minutes for my breath to return to normal and my vision to come back. Jack's face was pressed against my neck and his heart still thudded rapidly against my chest. I looked at the ring he'd placed on my finger and then kissed him lightly on the top of the head as I smiled.

"You're thinking pretty loud," he mumbled. "If you can think right now I didn't do my job."

"I'm not naming the cardiovascular system in alphabetical order if that's what you're implying."

"Well thank God for that." He lifted slightly so he looked down into my eyes, a smile tilting the corner of his mouth.

"I was just thinking that I'm happy. And I was admiring my ring. It looks good on me."

"You know what else looks good on you?" he asked.

My grin was wide and foolish in answer to the laughter in his eyes. "What?"

"Me." He leaned in to kiss me, this time soft and slow and without the frantic need that had consumed us before. But the heat still simmered between us. "I'm going to attempt to get us both to the bed, but you have to swear to not laugh if my legs give out."

"We could just sleep here," I suggested. I gasped and arched as he moved against me, thick and hard once more.

"I've got more than sleeping on my mind at the moment."

"I can feel that. But you've got to do all the work this time. I'm exhausted."

I watched in pure female admiration as he wrapped his arm beneath my back and lifted me, the muscles in his arms and shoulders bulging beneath my fingertips.

"Maybe you'll get your second wind soon."

My back hit the cool comforter on the bed and I cried out as he sent me over the edge. "I could probably be talked into it," I panted.

"You know how I love a challenge." He moved again and I was lost.

———

A COUPLE of hours later my mind and body were refreshed and I wanted to work. The hotel room was making me go stir crazy.

"We need to get back home," I said. "I need to look at the autopsy reports again. There's something there that I've missed and it's bothering me."

Jack had pulled on a pair of lounge pants and sat propped up in the bed with his laptop, going over some new information Carver had sent over.

"We'll be back home in a few hours," he said absentmindedly. "Carver sent me the file on Paris Spencer. It looks like the Lieber boys weren't the only ones who were smarter than their own good. Spencer attended the same boarding school in England as the Liebers, Parker and Anderson. They formed their circle early on in their childhood and according to the file, they didn't allow anyone new to intrude on their friendship. It was a closed circle, but it was also extremely competitive."

"They stayed within fractions of points of each other on their academics, and according to the file their competitiveness extended to outside of the classroom as well. Their junior year of high school, there were a series of explosions across campus."

"You said there was an explosives expert when we first talked to Greer."

"I'm getting to that. The explosions started off small. The first in the boys' bathroom. No injuries, and it got classes cancelled for the week while there was an investigation. The surveillance cameras had been messed with so no suspects."

"The next was a little larger in scale and happened about six months later, still in the middle of junior year. The advanced chemistry lab was leveled two days before exams. And this time there was a casualty. The professor went up with it, and most of his body parts were found. His name was Thomas Atkins."

"Nice," I said, grimacing as I looked over Jack's shoulder at the crime scene photos.

"The investigators found traces of unstable compounds and it was decided that the professor must have made a mistake in an experiment he was working on. There was nothing else found in the rubble that would suggest it was a device of any kind."

"But when we dug a little further we found that Jordan Parker and Eric Lieber were on probation for cheating. They were to go before an advisory board and Dr. Atkins was going to present his evidence against them and push for expulsion as well as failing his class, which would make them have to retake it the next year."

"Handy. Get rid of the teacher and he can't testify against you."

"Exactly. But nothing could be proven. Only suspicion. Next we've got another explosion only two months later. Classes were dismissed for a study break for four days, and most students went home. Because of distance the group converged on Peter Anderson's home since he had a home closest to the school.

"This is where things start to click," Jack said. "While on holiday some friend of a friend had a party. Adam Boxer was an American soldier on leave for three weeks, and he winds up at this party that was a friend of a friend of Anderson's."

I raised my brows as the *Ahh* moment hit. "And Boxer and Paris Spencer hit it off."

"That's the polite way of saying it. Friends say they started off hot and heavy from the moment they met. In fact, witnesses say they hooked up in one of the guest rooms about half an hour after they met. Paris Spencer went back to Boxer's place shortly after that, and when the holiday was over and everyone returned back to school, she was a no show."

"The school called her parents, but they couldn't be reached for several days. Spencer spent the remaining time of Boxer's leave with him until the police showed up almost two weeks later to escort her back to campus on her parents' orders. She didn't go willingly, and because she missed so much class and several key exams she ended up flunking that quarter."

"Three days after Spencer was escorted back to class the lead officer who came and took her away from Boxer was killed in an explosion in his home along with his wife and three children. The cops looked at Boxer hard, but he was alibied tight for the time in question, and he eventually went back to active duty."

"Things stayed quiet for the rest of the school year and until they all graduated. Then we see the same kind of thing start about the time they all enter university together. Same deal. They don't like to be separated from each other and end up attending the same university, though their majors are all very different. There were three more explosions that went unsolved during their tenure at university, and each of the victims had somehow done something wrong in their eyes or they'd felt they'd been slighted in some way."

"But nothing was ever proven," I said. "What happened with Boxer?"

"Every time he has leave he spends it with Spencer, and when his last tour was up he turned in his retirement papers and went to join her. They never married but they were together up until his death during the heist. She was questioned extensively, but it was postponed because she had to be hospitalized and sedated when she got the word of Boxer's death. She spent more than a year in a mental institution, uncommunicative. Investigators never could get in to question her, and by the time a year had passed there wasn't really any point because the case had been closed."

"We need to talk to Paris Spencer." I ran my fingers through my hair and blew out a breath of frustration.

"Yeah, we need to talk to Paris Spencer. But Carver says she's in France and the chances of getting her here are slim. She hasn't set foot in America since Boxer was killed, though fresh flowers show up on his grave once a month."

"We need to go back tonight, Jack. Wake up Carver and tell him he can either drive us back or we're taking a cab." I pulled off the tank and boxers I'd put on to sleep in and grabbed clothes out of my bag.

"It can't wait five hours?"

"I missed something. I need to look at those photographs again."

He sighed and closed his computer. "You've got that look on your face, so I'm not going to try and argue. Let me call Carver and see what he wants to do."

I nodded and put on jeans and a Georgetown University sweatshirt. I didn't much care what Carver wanted to do. I was going back to Virginia tonight whether he wanted me to or not.

17

"MY WIFE HAS SOME CHOICE WORDS TO SAY TO YOU, JACK," Carver said once we were back on the road. "The baby was actually asleep and there wasn't a toddler between us in the bed. Do you realize how rare that is? Not to mention she got her six week report back and she was all in the clear."

"I don't mean to let murder interrupt your sex life."

"And if things get violent when she has those words with you I'm not going to do anything to stop it. I'll just stand back and watch. And I'll enjoy it, you bastard."

"Would you be this cranky if you weren't getting to have sex with me?" I asked Jack, curiously.

"I wouldn't know. I haven't had to go without, and the couple rounds we had earlier will probably hold me through tomorrow."

"I hate you," Carver said, making my lips twitch. "You just wait until you have kids. Maybe I'll go poke holes in all your condoms just to help you along."

"You've got issues, Carver. I have no idea what the FBI psych profiler would have to say about that."

"He'd say I need to get laid. Why was it again that we needed to leave in the middle of the night?"

"There's something that's been bothering me about the autopsy reports on Jack's men. I need to study them closer. In particular, I need to study the reports on Andrew Caine a little closer. Something isn't right there."

The drive back to Bloody Mary seemed to take forever and I tapped my fingers against my leg and stared out into the darkness while Jack and Carver talked up front. I noticed the tail as soon as we crossed into King George County.

"It's Donaldson," Carver said. "He's going to follow us in. Greer was able to pin down a location for Jesse Tydell while we were gone. He's got undercover agents keeping an eye on him. We're hoping he'll make contact with other members of the gang and we can take them all."

"The gang members are the killers," I said. "We know that without a doubt. But they acted as the weapons. They're just a small part of the puzzle. The gang is the metaphorical bullet but someone else is pulling the trigger. Whoever that is is just as guilty of murder as the Vagos gang."

Carver sighed. "Right. We just have to find them first. I'm going to see what I can do about bringing in Paris Spencer. We need to talk to her."

Donaldson's lights were bright behind us as we finally made our way into Bloody Mary. Nerves dampened the palms of my hands, and I dried them quickly on my jeans. I didn't like the thought that there could be someone out there watching and waiting for Jack right now. Our home was supposed to be safe, but it didn't feel that way anymore. I wouldn't breathe easier until we were inside with the doors locked behind us.

It only took another ten minutes or so until the house came into view. Carver parked in the garage and we went in through the mudroom door, but I didn't wait on them to do a walkthrough of the house. I went straight to the offices and to the table where I'd been combing through the autopsy reports.

"Just give me a minute," I said, when they came in behind me. "I just need some quiet."

"Carver and I will be in the kitchen making coffee." And they left me alone.

I lined up the crime scene photos next to each other on the table and put the reports beneath them, reading through them all again. I saved Caine's until last and by that time I knew what had been bothering me.

"Jack," I called out.

"We're here," he said. I hadn't even realized they'd been back in the room sitting at their own tables. He handed me a cup of coffee but I put it aside.

"We've got eight murders if you take out Elliott, who Jack killed during the heist, and Winters who died in the car crash. Those are the only two anomalies." I took a second to group them together. "We've got Wallace, Santos, and Gonzales with the same cause of death. Two gunshot wounds to the back of the head with a large caliber weapon. Testing proved that it came from a .357 Magnum with hollow point bullets. I don't know the results of Wallace's findings yet, but that was my assumption when I worked on his body. The weapon is going to be a match among all three. One killer took them out.

"Next we've got Dreyer and Thompson." I grouped their pictures together and then added Wolfe's next to them. "We've got the same thing here. Same cause of death for Dreyer and Thompson, and the same attempt that happened with Wolfe earlier today. Long range shots from a sniper rifle. The shots were taken by someone highly skilled, and they were kill shots. We got lucky today with Braddock and Wolfe. The weapon and caliber of the bullet are the same. This is going to be Jesse Tydell's work. He's your marksman.

"Moving on to the next group." I arranged the next two pictures together. "We've got Price and Garfield with the same cause of death. Slit throat. A fluid motion from left to right, severing the jugular at the entry point. The wound was deep, indicating the strength of the killer, and the angle of the wound indicates the assailant was around the same height as Price and a couple of inches taller than Garfield. He was also right handed since it was a left to right motion."

I grabbed a step stool and moved behind Carver to demonstrate.

"Oh, man. I hate being the test dummy."

"Be thankful I'm not using real props." I grabbed him by the hair and pulled his neck back to expose his throat. "It had to have been fast, considering the size of the victims. Come up behind them out of the blue. It's a skill. And the depth of the wound showed how strong the killer was. The knife nicked the C4 vertebra in both victims, almost taking their heads off. So you've got gang member number three as the killer here. They all have their own MOs."

"What about Caine?" Jack asked. "His throat was slit too."

I went back to the table and my photos. "It sure was, but not like Garfield and Price. Caine was found dead in a motel in the Trinidad area of DC. That's a bad part of town, and word was that Caine was supposed to meet with an informant. He was found in the bed, stripped of all clothing, with his throat slit and other shallow hack marks along the torso. His wallet and any valuables were missing from the scene. No fingerprints, and there's so much DNA in a room like that it wouldn't be admissible anyway."

"I feel like I'm missing something obvious," Carver said.

"The wound doesn't match," I said, showing the crime scene photo of Caine. "It's a shallower slice, nowhere near close enough to nick vertebra. And see how there's a jagged edge in the flesh here and here?" I pointed to the two offending spots. "The assailant wasn't nearly as strong. It was a struggle to tear through the arteries and nick the jugular. It wasn't even severed all the way, but it was enough for him to bleed out. This was done face to face, in very close contact."

"Damn," Jack said, crossing his arms over his chest. "It was a woman. Crime of passion, and in the middle of it too. Poor bastard."

"They didn't finish," I said, nodding. "Vaginal fluid was found and collected for DNA but tests show they didn't finish the deed. Not only was it a crime of passion, but she was majorly pissed. See these shallow wounds in the chest? These happened perimortem. She would've been covered in blood from head to toe."

"Do you think there's a chance Paris Spencer had a connection with Caine?" Jack asked.

"I know she did," Carver said, going back to his own table and rifling through stacks of paper. "Before Spencer had her nervous breakdown there was a police report filed by some of Caine's neighbors. Caine was the only one of the team interviewed on television after Boxer and the others were killed. It seems Paris tracked him down and there was some kind of altercation before the police arrived. She disappeared before the police got there, and Caine didn't know who she was at the time—only that she was a young woman, late twenties or early thirties, with long straight blond hair and blue eyes. Cops were stretched thin so when Paris tried to slit her wrists less than an hour later the connection wasn't made until she'd already been admitted to psych lockdown.

"This is good stuff, Doc. Enough that I can have Paris Spencer transported across international waters for questioning."

"The knife wound moved from right to left," I said.

"Left-handed killer. Paris Spencer is left handed." Carver smiled. "That information was almost worth missing a night of hot sex for. I'll alert Greer and we'll meet here first thing in the morning for a briefing."

"Then we'd better get some sleep," Jack said, taking my hand and pulling me toward the door. "Have I ever told you how hot it makes me to watch that brain of yours work?" He leaned down and kissed the sensitive spot below my ear.

"Oh, man. Why don't you just rub it in?" Carver complained. "If I hear sex noises coming from your room tonight, I'm going to start shooting through the wall and hope it hits you."

"Don't worry. I'll make sure to keep her mouth occupied." I snorted out a laugh and Jack tossed me over his shoulder and ran up the stairs.

18

THE ALARM WENT OFF AT HALF PAST FIVE AND I GROANED and buried my head under the pillow, pretending it would go away.

"Rise and shine, Doc."

"I've never understood how you can be so cheerful in the mornings without coffee."

"It's a gift. I have many."

I snorted out a laugh and threw off the covers. It was still dark outside, but the house would be swarming with agents before much longer. I sat up on the side of the bed and stretched, rotating my neck to alleviate the stiffness. There hadn't been much time for sleep the last two days.

Jack was already showered and dressed and he sat down next to me. "Let me see your back."

I turned and then let out a moan as his fingers worked magic up and down my spine and between my shoulder blades.

"That right there is totally worth marrying you for," I said between moans.

"That's not what you said last night." His hands snaked around and palmed my breasts before going back to the massage.

"Well, maybe I can think of a couple other reasons."

"Do you want breakfast?"

"It depends. Are you making it?"

"Well, I want to not die of food poisoning or have to rebuild my kitchen if you burn it down, so yes, I'm making it."

"In that case, I'd love some breakfast. And a pot of coffee."

"What are you going to do when there's a coffee shortage in the world and you have to do without?"

"I'm going to expect my rich husband to pay whatever he has to so I don't kill anyone when I wake up in the mornings without it."

"You're very violent without your caffeine. It's very sexy."

"I only have to breathe for you to think it's sexy."

"You speak the truth," he winked. "Grab your shower and meet me downstairs before I make us both late."

He slipped out of the bedroom and closed the door behind him, and I realized I had a ridiculous smile on my face. I rolled my eyes and headed to the bathroom to get ready for the day.

It was foolish of me, but I knew Lauren would be joining us for the meeting so I took more time with my appearance than normal. I blow dried my hair so it lay smooth around my face and I messed with my eyes some to make them look bigger, more exotic, and put a hint of color in my cheeks.

There was no point in trying to compete with her in the wardrobe department. My closet consisted of old comfortable jeans and T-shirts and business suits I wore at the funeral parlor. Expensive clothes were wasted in my profession because so many got ruined if I had to go to a crime scene or while I was doing an embalming.

I selected gray slacks and a purple wrap shirt that made it look like I had more boobs than I actually did, and then I sighed as I tried to decide on footwear. There was no point strangling my feet in icepick heels. I needed to be practical, and there was no way I could go a whole day wearing them without falling on my face. I decided on flat black half-boots I'd gotten on clearance the summer before and figured that was as good as it was going to get.

I went downstairs without a backward glance at the mirror and headed toward the smell of coffee and bacon.

"Good timing," Jack said, turning from the stove. His eyebrows raised at the sight of me and I felt self-conscious all of a sudden. I almost turned around and went back upstairs to wipe the stupid makeup off and change clothes, but Jack got that look in his eye that made my skin tingle.

He took the pan off the stove and turned the burner off and then walked toward me. No, stalked would be more accurate.

"I like that shirt. A lot. I especially like what's underneath it."

"You've seen what's underneath it a thousand times."

"That doesn't mean I ever get tired of it." His hands curved around my waist and he kissed me.

"Am I interrupting something?" Carver said from the doorway.

"No—"

"Yes—" Jack said.

"I smelled bacon. If you'd like, the two of you can just keep doing what you're doing and I'll eat all the bacon. Seems like a fair trade."

"If you eat all that bacon, your wife is going to have your head," Jack said, releasing me with a final kiss on the forehead. He went directly to the coffee pot and poured me a cup, handing it over as I took a seat on one of the barstools.

"She'll be able to smell it on me for days," Carver agreed, shaking his head sadly. "This is what marriage does to you. No sex and no bacon. It's just not right."

My lips twitched as a plate of eggs, bacon, and fluffy biscuits and gravy were put in front of me. "Maybe you should try to combine the two. It sounds like what you need are better time management skills."

"I'm not going to lie," Carver said, chewing thoughtfully. "The thought of combining those two things is very appealing. If I could have sports playing on the TV in the background it would be even better."

"Carver, I have a favor to ask." I pushed my plate away and fisted my hands in my lap.

"This sounds serious." He looked between me and Jack, but Jack stayed silent and let me do the talking.

"Very serious."

I took in a deep breath but it didn't really help. I knew my father was guilty of a lot of things, but it still felt like what I was about to do was some kind of betrayal. But I didn't want anyone else to get hurt. Especially me.

"I know that you have a job to do and I don't want to take advantage of your friendship, but I have some items that I'd like you to look into. Discretely, if possible. I know you won't be able to keep it a secret from the FBI, but I'd like you to be the one to look at them. Maybe it's not as bad as I think it will be and I'm overreacting. But I have to make sure."

"This is about your father?" he asked, going very still. "Why would I have interest in a dead man? Sometimes it's best to leave things buried, Jaye. But you didn't hear that bit of advice from me."

"Believe me, I wish I could."

I realized maybe it was best not to say anything about my father's return from the grave. Especially since that guilt was gnawing a hole in my stomach. He was still my dad, blood not withstanding. I could give him the flash drives and wait and see if what was on them made my father a current threat. I looked at Jack and realized by the look he was giving me that he'd already deduced what I was going to do. He shrugged and left the decision up to me.

I realized I wasn't only doing this for me, but I was doing it for Jack as well. Jack believed in the law. And if I kept this hidden and something bad happened because I didn't speak up when I should have it would drive a wedge between us that could never be repaired.

"I found some things that belonged to my father. A few flash drives. Jack says they're encrypted, so I thought you might be the best person to look at them."

Carver sighed. "There's a separate team of agents who have been working the case on your parents for the last couple of years. Technically, anything related to the case should go to them."

"I know. I've met those agents up close and personal, and it'll be a cold day in hell before I ever step into their path again after the way they treated me. I'm giving them to you because it's the right thing to do. But if I don't have another option I'd just as soon throw them in the fire than hand them over to anyone else. I need to know what's on there. What if the information could save a life?"

"And what am I supposed to do if I find something bad on those flash drives? I can't keep it from the agent in charge of the case. And don't expect there to not be anything on those flash drives. They wouldn't be encrypted if there wasn't a good reason." Carver pushed back his plate and got to his feet. Carver wasn't one to get agitated or have a bad mood for long. He used good humor and jokes to deal with the terrible things he saw in his line of work.

"I know that," I said softly. "I wouldn't expect you to. I want to give them to you because I trust you. I know Malachi and Angela Graves are just another set of criminals to you. They're nothing more than names with a thick file. But they were my parents. I just want to know what was on those flash drives, and if I have more to worry about once you find out."

"You totally ruined my bacon experience," Carver said, pouting a little. He sighed and slapped me on the back good-naturedly. "I'll look at them. And I'll give you a heads up once I turn the information over to the team in charge. But if you want some free advice from me, it might be best if you and Jack take a nice long honeymoon. Somewhere tropical maybe."

"Thanks, Ben. I mean it."

"I'd say anytime, but next time you find something like those flash drives you should probably go with your gut and throw them in the fire."

A knock sounded at the door and Jack pushed his plate back. "That'll be Greer and the other agents. Looks like it's time to get started."

"I'll get it," I said. "You get the flash drives for Carver."

I went to the front door and opened it for Agent Greer. Lauren Rhodes stood beside him along with Donaldson, and two agents I hadn't seen before, but I was surprised to see Sam Wolfe in their midst. I checked his color and his pupils automatically. He was a little pale, but he seemed to be standing on his own okay.

I stood aside and they all filed in and headed to the office. Jack and Carver came in behind us.

"How's Agent Braddock?" I asked Greer.

"Thanks to you, he's alive. He's still in critical condition, but they think his chances look good. Carver tells me you had a bit of a breakthrough last night with the autopsy reports. Why don't you go through it for us, and then I'll give an update on my end."

Carver had found an empty board from somewhere for my

use, and I started tacking up the pictures in the groupings I'd put them in the night before. I explained what I'd found about the three methods of killing and the three different killers. And then I explained the difference in Andrew Caine's murder.

"So what we have here is tiers of killing," I said. "We've got three members of the Vagos. Hired killers with three different methods—execution style shots to the head, a deep cut across the throat with a smooth edged blade, and a long-range sniper. I read the reports on the Vagos and it's a competition to them for status and ranking within the organization. That's why you have the varying methods and multiple killers. Jesse Tydell is your sniper."

"And he's going to be the most dangerous because you can't see him," Lauren said. She leaned back against the wall and crossed her arms over her chest while she was thinking. "The other two like it up close and personal. They like the hunt and overpowering their victim before they use their method of killing to end their life."

"Exactly," I said, nodding.

"And then we have killer number four with Caine," Jack said. "Different MO. Evidence points to a woman. This was a crime of passion, also up close and personal, but for a different reason. There was anger in this kill. We need to find out everything we can about Caine's personal life. All the women he's dated or been seen with."

"That could take years," Carver said. "The man liked his women."

"Then start with whoever was most current and work backwards. Women usually know if the man they're sleeping with is also hopping beds with others."

"Do we have names of Jesse Tydell's Vagos associates?" I asked. "Those that fit the kill descriptions?"

"We sure do," Greer said. He tacked two more photographs up on the criminal board. "Lester Grimm served in the Gulf War with Tydell and was recruited into the Vagos by him. Grimm lost his entire troop in a convoy that was bombed and he was left for dead. He had severe brain trauma and lost partial hearing. He spooks at the sound of gunfire, so his weapon of choice is a stainless steel Buck Knife with a nine-inch blade. We haven't had a sighting of Grimm in more than a year, but I have a feeling he's close by. Jack and Wolfe are the last kills on their list. Like Doctor Graves said, it's a competition and they're in it to win. Our profiler report says that the addition of federal agents and heightened police awareness will only add points to their game."

Greer pinned a second picture on the board next to Grimm. This one was a formal shot of an officer in dress blues. A handsome man with a serious look on his face as he posed for the shot. "This is Greg Lassiter. He was an illegals detective in LA. Worked undercover for a while, but it went south. His wife and daughter were murdered because of it, and the Internal Affairs investigation discovered there was a leak on the inside in Lassiter's department and the mole handed over Lassiter and his family to the dealers.

"Lassiter killed the cop responsible and then went off the grid. He was prime pickings for the Vagos, considering his disillusionment for law enforcement. He moved up the ranks quickly and was sent to head up his own territory in Chicago. The .357 Magnum he uses to kill his victims is symbolic.

When he was on the force back in the 90s, that was his service revolver.

"Grimm, Lassiter, and Tydell are all gang territory leaders in their cities. This competition likely means there is a position open for a new general, and they're fighting for it. They won't take each other out, because there's honor involved here. It's the law enforcement and military background that makes them want to win above board."

"That is completely fucked up," Carver said.

I was a visual learner so I drew a pyramid on my white board and divided it into three sections. At the bottom of the pyramid I put Tydell, Grimm, and Lassiter along with the men they'd killed thus far. In the middle slot of the pyramid I put Caine's name and mystery woman. At the top of the pyramid I put "Money Man." Whoever controlled the money was the one we weren't having any luck finding.

Greer's phone rang and he frowned as he looked at the caller ID. "Greer," he said, and then immediately came to his feet. "We're on our way." He motioned for his agents to follow him.

"We've lost sight of Jesse Tydell," he said, explaining. "We watched him go into his motel room last night and lock in, but that was the last sighting. The two agents who were watching him are dead and Tydell's disappeared. Jack, I want you and Wolfe to stay locked up tight here." Greer followed his agents out of the house, slamming the door behind him.

Fear curdled in my belly and I moved beside Jack, just to be close to him. Too many people had died at the hands of these men, and I was terrified there would be more before it was over. I was starting to think leaving the country for a little while might not be a bad idea. My second thought was even worse. That maybe it wouldn't be so bad to ask for my dad's help.

Jack took my hand and squeezed it. "They're going to be busy for a while. The least we can do is wade through all the paperwork. Let's talk financials, Carver."

Carver nodded and moved to his computer, taking a little time to set it up so it projected on the wall for everyone to see. "After speaking with Mrs. Lieber yesterday I started doing some research into that support group she told us about. Wives and Mothers of the Fallen—WMF. It's a protected organization, similar to abuse shelters, so that names or donors are all considered anonymous. There's a database, but we'd need a warrant to go through the listing."

"You've got to get me something concrete before I can request a warrant for those names," Lauren said. "WMF isn't under suspicion for anything."

"No, but we know that the Liebers have donated hundreds of thousands of dollars to this organization, and they're under suspicion."

"It still won't be enough for me to violate the privacy of all those other women. Keep looking and come up with more and I'll be happy to take it to a judge."

Carver sighed and muttered under his breath, "Lawyers." He moved to a different screen. "See if this does anything for you. Paris Spencer is a member of the same organization. She also makes significant donations, though she's never attended a meeting or a charity function since they all take place stateside. I need a list of all the members. That's going to be where we find the connection between friends and family of the victims.

WMF's donations are open records, though they don't have names listed next to the amounts. This is a billion dollar charity."

"From what I understand, the money is allocated to those women who were not left with life insurance policies or were denied benefits for some reason or another. Or if they lose their jobs, they can make a claim through the charity like they would for unemployment. Right now I'm having to go through individual financial records of every relative and friend of all of these victims to see if there are similar donations. I need that warrant."

"With both Spencer and Mrs. Lieber making considerable contributions I could probably spin it in our favor. Let me see what I can do." Lauren took out her cell phone and left the room, leaving me, Carver, Jack, and Wolfe to look at the murder boards.

"Let's check phone records and email from both Mrs. Lieber and Spencer," Carver said. "We'll see if they've had any contact for the last six years."

"How the hell did all this happen, Jack?" Wolfe asked. "It was a mission just like any other. No more dangerous than any other job we did. Now I find out Elliott was dirty and he's the one who shot you? It just doesn't make sense."

Wolfe slouched back on the sofa, the white bandage covering his wound peeking out from his T-shirt. Confusion and anger and sadness marred his features.

"He had his reasons," Jack said. "His actions were understandable, even though there had to be a better way. His child was going to die, Sam. I'm not sure there's anything he wouldn't have done to keep her alive."

Jack paced back and forth in front of the boards and got a look in his eyes I was all too familiar with. He loved the thrill of the chase and the adrenaline that pumped through his veins as the puzzle pieces began to fit together.

"Dig deeper into that charity that Jane Elliott mentioned to us. The one that funded her daughter's surgery. That money had to come from somewhere. Who's on the board of directors? Is it private or a public funded organization?"

"On it," Carver said, heading to his laptop, his fingers flying over the keys. "There are layers here that are going to take some time."

"Well, we've got good news and bad news," Lauren said, her heels clicking on the hardwood as she came back in. "Wives and Mothers of the Fallen has top notch lawyers. I got a judge to grant a warrant, but they're blocking it based on privacy laws. We need more information. What we know for certain is that a gang is responsible for the deaths of nine men. We don't have a suspect for anyone controlling the purse strings, even though we know that's what's happening. And the WMF attorneys are using that to block the warrant. We can't invade the lives of hundreds of women who are basically victims without probable cause. So get me probable cause and I can bury them and all the paper they're generating while trying to stall."

"I hope that's the bad news," Jack said.

"It was," Lauren nodded. "The good news is we had an agent on personal leave in France, and he's going to go back on active duty and escort Paris Spencer back to the United States for questioning."

"I'm glad it's not only my vacations that get interrupted," Jack said.

Lauren smiled but it reminded me of a shark just before biting into its prey. "She'll be here in a few hours. Greer will want to question her. I'd like to hear what she has to say myself, but I need to stay here."

"Because the Vagos are your priority?" Jack asked.

"Don't get on your high and mighty pedestal, Jack. These men will be an asset to have in our pockets."

"Because it's always good to let murderers, especially murderers of cops, go free so the Justice Department can think they're in control. Let me guess, you guys are in bed with Homeland Security on this one?"

"There are facets to this job. You know that." The frustration in her voice was evident, and I had a feeling this was an argument they'd had before. "You see everything in black and white. But that's not the way the world works."

"Mostly because politicians, lawyers, and bureaucrats tie up the system with red tape and bullshit so they can one up each other. What if Tydell or the others fire on more officers and we have a shot? Are we just supposed to walk away and let it happen?"

"Shoot to incapacitate. Not to kill. Those are your orders."

"It's a lot easier giving orders having never stood in the line of fire, sweetheart," Wolfe said. "I say we give you a vest and put you out there to defend your life and the lives of others and see if you shoot to incapacitate."

"You're trying to make me out as the monster here, when you

know having men like this under our thumb will save count-less lives in the long run. I am on your side. But I have a job to do and I'm going to make sure it gets done."

"I hope you never have to experience standing over the graves of the people whose lives you and the Justice Department are playing with." Jack turned his back to Lauren so he stared at the faces of each of his men on the white board. "It's not good for the soul. Believe me on that."

Everyone settled down at their tables with a stack of files to wade through, and I slipped out of the room to get more coffee now that things had settled down a bit. I looked out the kitchen window in the trees and wondered if there was anyone out there. If Tydell was waiting and watching for his moment. I didn't have a lot of faith in the FBI to protect us, my past experience with my parents withstanding.

I turned when I heard the familiar click of heels come into the room. "I just came in for more coffee," she said, going to the pot. "Jack always did make really good coffee."

I didn't know what to say so I stayed silent and turned to face her completely, leaning back against the counter.

"I don't want to make things awkward, but I'm assuming you know that Jack and I have a bit of a past."

"He told me." My lips twitched as I looked her in the eye. "Jack has had a lot of pasts."

She smiled and tipped her cup to me. "That he has. I wasn't sure when I saw the two of you together that you were a good fit for him. He's a good man and he deserves to be happy. To have someone who can give him that and understand him at the same time. Jack's more complicated than he seems to most people."

"He certainly is." I had no idea where this was going. I didn't know if Lauren was about to make her pitch for why she would be better suited or suggest that I do what was best for Jack and bow out of the picture. I only knew that I really liked the kitchen and would hate to get blood on anything if I had to kill her.

"He talked about you, you know? Back when we were together."

My eyebrows raised at that bit of information. Jack had never mentioned Lauren to me. Hadn't even told me he was living with someone, and we'd been just as close then as we'd always been. Though our conversations had mostly been through email and phone calls. We'd been too busy to see each other much.

"I was jealous if you want to know the truth. He always had stories about Jaye," she said, smiling. "The things you did together or the practical jokes you played on each other. He worried about you living in the city alone and in the part of town where your apartment was. I heard the love in his voice every time he mentioned your name. I wanted that, and I hated you for it even though I'd never met you."

"I'm sorry," I said softly. I could empathize with her. I couldn't imagine how I'd feel if it were the other way around.

She shrugged it away. "I realized after we moved in together that it wouldn't work between us. Don't get me wrong," she grinned. "We were very compatible in certain ways. Jack is very—talented."

"You probably don't want to go there." I felt the heat rising to my cheeks. I knew *exactly* what she was talking about. Talented was an understatement.

"But we were both too headstrong, and as you saw back there, we see things very differently. My career will always come first, and Jack may not realize it, but he needs the kind of person who will always put him first. And he'll need to do the same to whoever he ends up with."

"Are you trying to scare me away or encourage me to stay?" I asked curiously.

"I don't know. Maybe a little of both. Like I said, I wasn't sure you were the one for him yesterday when I first saw you together. There was tension and something else standing between you. But I've been watching you together. I don't even think you realize what you have. It's like watching a dance whenever you're in the same room together. You know what he wants and are able to give it to him before he does and vice versa. You have this unspoken communication and your bodies are in sync. You're his world. I can see that now. The little touches or the looks he gives you when you don't realize he's watching. It's a beautiful thing to see. And I find myself just as jealous of what you have now as what you had then. Congratulations on your upcoming marriage. I truly hope you're very happy."

The lump in my throat made it difficult to speak. I wasn't sure I could have shown the same generosity and kindness if our positions had been reversed. "Thank you. I appreciate that very much. If it makes you feel better, I'm extremely jealous of your shoes."

She laughed and stuck out her leg so the icepick heel she

seemed to prefer—this one in vivid red—could be seen. "They are pretty fabulous. And unlike men, shoes are never a disappointment. I actually came in here to talk about something else, though I guess I needed to get the other off my chest first."

"What is it?"

"Jack is wasted here, you must know that."

"I do, but it's Jack's decision. He'll make a change if he wants to and if he's ready."

"The FBI has wanted him for years. There's a reason he and Carver are such good buddies. They've been trying to recruit him for almost a decade. He's been through several special training sessions at Quantico. His intelligence is very high and he has the physical skills as well."

"I thought he had issues with authority. Isn't that bad in the FBI? No offense, but with the exception of Carver all these other agents seem like drones."

"There are many aspects of the FBI. Not everyone is cut from the same cloth. And they like agents who think outside the box—mostly. He belongs in the field. He's too good at what he does."

"It's not my decision, but I'll support whatever choice he makes."

"But you could certainly help influence him. What if I told you there's an opening in the medical examiner's office in DC?"

"I'd say that doesn't have much to do with me. I'm not a

licensed pathologist. I'm just a coroner with a medical degree."

"It'd be a training position while you got your certification. Full pay with benefits. Reliable pay."

She struck a chord there. To say my current position was reliable would be a lie. I was able to pay bills solely based on how many people died per month. And I had *a lot* of bills. Hundreds of thousands of dollars in student loan debt from medical school.

"And you're suggesting all this out of the goodness of your heart?"

"I never do anything out of the goodness of my heart. I've been accused more than once of not even having one. But what I am good at is my job. And I want the people I work with on a frequent basis to be good at their job too. Jack would be an asset to the agency. He'd be using his talents for something other than writing parking tickets for speeding livestock. Just think about it."

"Thanks, I will."

She nodded and left to go back with the others. Did I want to work in the medical examiner's office? Not particularly. I didn't really enjoy working with the dead. I'd always preferred the living. But I didn't hate it. And I knew I'd do it if Jack wanted to make the move and join the FBI. It was definitely something to think about.

19

"THAT WAS GREER," CARVER SAID, HANGING UP THE PHONE A short time later. "Agents found the body of Greg Lassiter in the motel room Tydell was holed up in. A maid found him when she went in to clean. He was shot through the head with his own weapon. The gun was left on site, and they're checking to see if it's a match for Wallace, Santos, and Gonzales."

"That's my cue to go," Lauren said, gathering her briefcase. "I need to see the scene and see if there are any leads on the others."

"I thought you said there was a code of honor," Wolfe said. "That they wouldn't kill each other because there was a code."

"It looks like the rules changed." Lauren waved goodbye and then left out the front door.

Wolfe whistled and grinned. "She might be irritating, but she has some damn fine legs."

"I thought you had a girlfriend," I said, remembering she'd been questioned after his disappearance.

"Honey, I always have girlfriends, and Lawyer Rhodes is going to be added to the list."

"Fifty bucks says she turns him down flat," Carver said.

Jack's head was buried in papers and it didn't look like he was paying much attention. "That's a sucker's bet."

"You all forget that I'm wounded. Women love a guy that's been hurt in the line of duty. She'll be all over me."

"Like a rash," I said dryly.

"What have you got there, Jack?" Carver asked. I looked at Jack and realized he'd gotten very still as he read through one of the financial reports.

"Son of a bitch," he said. "The WMF sent payments for almost two years to Jane Elliott. And look here." He picked up another stack of papers and highlighted the amounts. "Payments for six months sent to the mother of Adam Boxer. We'll find both of their names on the member roster. I almost missed it because the payments were direct deposit on the fifteenth of the month, and it's the exact same amount as her widow's benefits, which she received on the first of every month. There's no description of who the sender is, just a twelve digit numerical code. And the numerical code is one digit off from the code that the police department uses to make direct deposits. They'd have to have a hacker of some kind to get into the department payroll database and be able to set it up like that."

"Hackers leave signatures," Carver said. "Let me see if I can work backwards and find out where it's coming from."

"I need to talk to Jane Elliott again," Jack said. "Dammit." He rubbed his hands over his face. "Goddammit." He punched the wall hard enough for me to wince and wonder if he'd damaged his knuckles.

"She could still be innocent in this, Jack," I said, taking his hand and rubbing the sting out a bit. "If they came to her and offered her the money as a supplement why would she turn them down? A couple of years of payments would have gotten her back on her feet again, especially with all the medical bills she must have had during Katie's treatments."

He squeezed my hand and nodded, but I could tell he didn't really believe me. "I need to call her and set up a time to meet."

"Do you want me to do it?" Carver asked.

"No, she knows me. Trusts me. And I'll make sure she tells me everything." He took his cell phone from his pocket and left the room to make the call.

"This is going to be hard on him," I said. "He's felt responsible for her all these years because he was the one who pulled the trigger on her husband. If she's involved in this I'm going to be really pissed."

Wolfe tried stretching and started to lift his arm and then winced.

"Don't do that," I scolded. "You'll tear your stitches. How are you feeling?"

"Like I got shot in the shoulder. It's more irritating than anything. It's my shooting arm, so that's going to slow me down a little, but I'm proficient enough with my left hand."

I rolled my eyes. "Well then, we should put you out on the front lines so you can prove your manhood."

"Sweetheart, I can prove my manhood right here and now if you're that curious."

"Keep it in your pants, Wolfe," Jack said, coming back in the room. "Once she starts laughing, it's hard for her to stop."

"I'm probably going to have to punch you for that. Once I'm back to full strength of course."

"You can certainly try. Being a P.I. has probably turned you soft. I promise to put you down quickly and then we can go grab a beer."

"*Helloo*," I said. "Can we get back on track here? Were you able to get hold of Jane?"

"We're supposed to meet her at 11:00 at Coastal Flats up in Fairfax. We need to get moving if we're going to make it in time."

"Wait a second," Carver said. "There aren't any agents available to tail you at the moment. Let me make a call."

"We've got this. I know how to spot a tail and I'm armed."

"That's not going to do any good against a sniper rifle. Especially if Jane Elliott is involved in this. She could have eyes on her already."

"If she's got people watching her then that means she's the one in danger. You know this has to be done and I'm the only one to do it."

Jack looked at me and started to say something, but I cut him off. "Don't even think about it. I'm going with you. I happen to agree with Carver that you should wait for backup, but I know you and figure you'll ignore me just as well as you ignore him."

"We're going to be in a public place in the middle of the city. We'll be fine and back in a few hours."

"Do me a favor and keep your line open when you meet," Carver said. "If there's trouble I can have agents from the nearby office there in minutes."

"Will do. Let's go, Doc. You can watch my back."

"I'd rather watch your front, but I guess I'll take what I can get." Jack grinned and slung his arm around me while Wolfe and Carver laughed. I had a random thought as we headed toward the door.

"Hey, Wolfe. Do you have the tattoo?"

"I have many, but I'm assuming you mean the SWAT tattoo. The answer is yes. Each of us had it done as part of our initiation. You want to know where mine is?"

"I'm sure it's the same place as your manhood, but I don't have time to look for that either."

Carver and Jack hooted out a laugh and Wolfe scowled. "Damn, woman. That's just cruel. Why'd you want to know if you don't want to see it?"

"Because I just remembered that I didn't see a tattoo on Caine. I looked over ever inch of those autopsy photos. Are you sure everyone got the tattoo?"

"I know for a fact Caine got his. We came in at the same time. Did all of our testing together and were initiated at the same time. Remember, Jack?"

"I remember," Jack nodded. "Are you sure you didn't see it anywhere? If I remember right Caine's tattoo was just above his left shoulder blade."

I thought back to the autopsy photos, but I knew I wasn't mistaken. "No, I'm sure. He didn't have a tattoo anywhere. I'll look closer when we get back and see if I see any scarring from a removal."

"What if he doesn't have it?" Wolfe asked.

"Then we need to deal with the possibility that maybe the body in those photos isn't really Caine."

———

ELEVEN O'CLOCK WAS a good time to meet at Coastal Flats. It was right at opening time in the middle of the week and the place wasn't crowded like it would be in another hour or so. I spotted Jane as soon as we walked inside.

If anything she looked even thinner than the last time I'd seen her. Her face was pale and her lips thin. I don't know what Jack said to her over the phone, but she didn't look particularly happy to see us.

"Thanks for meeting us here, Jane," Jack said, leaning in carefully to hug her.

"You didn't give me a lot of choice. What's all this about? Is something wrong? Have you found out more about John's death? I really don't feel like getting out, and I've got a lot of work to do at home."

"Just relax," he said. "I'll explain everything in a minute."

The hostess came over to seat us and I was surprised at how

adamant Jane was about sitting indoors instead of out on the patio area. The weather was beautiful, but she seemed to shrink into herself even more at the thought of being out in the sunlight.

I hadn't known Jane Elliott for very long, but it didn't take a rocket scientist to realize that she needed psychological help. She'd been through a lot over the last six years, and from everything Jack had told me, the way she was acting now wasn't normal. She'd been fine. She'd learned to live as the widow of a good cop, and had been strong while raising her children and being there for the one who'd struggled to live.

This woman didn't look like the fighter I knew she was. She looked scared. And broken. The hostess sat us in a booth in the corner, and Jack sat with his back to the wall so he could see the front door and out the glass windows that went across the entire front. We ordered drinks and our food and got by on awkward small talk until they arrived.

"Tell me about Wives and Mothers of the Fallen," Jack said.

Jane bobbled the hot tea she'd ordered and then wrapped her hands tightly around the mug. "I—I'm not sure I understand."

"Jane," Jack said with a resigned sigh. "We know you received payments from them for two years after John died. Are you a member of the organization?"

"Obviously you already know the answer to that question since you've been through my financial records." Her shoulders straightened and she lifted her chin.

"Listen to me. I'm here to help you. I've always been here to help you. But you need to tell me the truth. The more we uncover about this organization, the more it appears they're not all they seem to be."

"They're exactly what they say they are. They help women who've lost their husbands or sons, and that includes financially. I would have lost the house if they hadn't stepped in after John died. I hadn't worked in years since I'd elected to stay home with the girls after they were born, and I spent every waking minute at the hospital with Katie once she got sick. The benefits after John's death came nowhere near to cutting it. I applied for membership to WMF and qualified for one of the grants they give out to those in need. Once I found a good paying position and I was back on my feet again, they stopped the payments."

"Do you know Paris Spencer?"

She shook her head no. "The FBI already asked me that. I've never heard of her."

"What about Grace Lieber?"

Jane looked away as she answered. "I recognize the name, but I don't know her. I believe she does a lot of the charity work with the foundation. Really, Jack, this is all ridiculous. They gave me money when I needed it. I don't know what you want me to say."

Jane was lying, and she wasn't very good at it. She picked up her fork and I felt a slow fissure of unease ripple through me. Jane Elliott was left-handed. I wasn't sure what made the thought pop into my head, but once it was there I couldn't get rid of it. So I tested the waters, hoping to catch her off guard.

"How long after John died did Andrew Caine start coming around?"

If possible her face paled even more and she moved quickly, trying to get out of the booth and run away, but Jack grabbed her wrist and held her in place. She didn't have the strength to struggle with him and she collapsed back in her seat and curled into herself.

"Jesus, Jane. It was you? You're the one who killed him?" Jack dropped her wrist and I could see he was honestly floored by the realization. This was his friend. Someone he thought he'd known.

She rocked back and forth and a sob escaped, though she tried to hold it in. A couple of other diners glanced our way, and Jane turned her face so she was looking at the wall. No wonder she wasn't looking good. The guilt of murder obviously weighed heavily on her.

"What am I going to do about my girls? What am I going to do?" The tears streamed down her cheeks and I wasn't sure she was really with us mentally anymore. It seemed like she'd gone to her own place.

"You need to tell me what happened. The truth and every bit of it this time. I can't help you if I don't know what's going on."

"I did it. I killed him."

Jack pushed her water glass toward her and she wrapped shaky hands around it, bringing it to her lips. "Just start at the beginning. When did you start having a relationship with Caine?"

Her voice was barely more than a whisper. "He started coming around after John died, kind of like you and a couple of the others did. He'd fix things around the house or run errands if I needed anything and was stuck at the hospital with Katie. He was just so nice and I started to rely on him to be there. Nothing happened between us for years because I was a mess after John died. But then one day I woke up and realized Andrew was there, and I finally saw him as something more than a friend."

"You loved him," I said.

She nodded and another tear slid down her cheek. "We became lovers, but something wasn't right. He was secretive and I knew he lied to me sometimes about the things he was doing or where he was going. He always said he was working and wouldn't tell me anything more, but I knew it was more than that.

"He asked me to meet him that day at the motel room. I thought he was trying to be romantic. I thought he might ask me to marry him." Her breath hitched and her lips trembled as she tried to get control of herself. "But he didn't. He said he was being followed and that it wasn't safe, so that's why we had to meet like that. Then he told me what he'd found out. He said that you killed John."

Jane's gaze bore into Jack's eyes as she said it, daring him to deny it. "Is it true?"

Jack didn't look away from her when he answered. "It's true."

"I slapped him when he told me that," she said. "Asked him why he was trying to hurt me with lies, but he wouldn't stop talking. He said John had been a traitor and that he'd been working with the men who'd tried to rob the bank.

"He started asking questions about WMF just like you did.

He knew about the payments they'd been giving me, and he wanted to know what they'd asked me to do in return. He asked me if I'd known what John had been involved in all along. If I knew that WMF had helped fund the operation that had killed John."

"He asked that specifically?" Jack asked.

She nodded without looking at Jack.

"And were they?"

"I didn't know that John was involved with those people. I swear I didn't. Not until after he died. Then they came to me and told me I was theirs now."

"Who came to you?"

"A woman named Genny Boxer. She said her son was killed with John during the robbery. She said I was theirs and I belonged to them now. That they'd be there for me during my grief and through the rest of it. And they said that I owed them because they'd saved Katie's life."

"Are you saying that WMF owns the Kids with Cancer charity?" I asked.

"I don't know if it's their charity, but I know that's where the anonymous donation came from and the instructions were that it had to go to us for Katie's treatment."

"Give me a second, Jane. You're doing the right thing." Jack took out his phone and hit a number for speed dial.

"Carver," he said once the call was connected. "You need to send someone to pick up Genny Boxer. She's the one who initially contacted Jane to meet. And dig harder into the Kids with Cancer Foundation. Jane confirms that the money came from WMF. See if it's just an offshoot of the same fund. We're going to need a safe house for Jane and her children. Get that set up too."

Jack was silent for a couple of seconds, listening to whatever it was Carver was saying on the other end and then he said goodbye.

The look on Jane's face was devastating. She'd heard about the safe house, and it was starting to sink in what a dangerous position she was in.

"Oh my God, Jack. They'll kill me. And the girls. You have to send someone to my mother's house right now. Have someone get them and take them away." Hysteria tinged her voice and the color seeped back into her face. Jane Elliott's children were her strength and it was coming back with a vengeance at the thought of them being hurt.

"It's already being taken care of," he said. "The FBI is sending agents as we speak to get the girls and your mother to a safe place. They'll take you as soon as we're done here."

"Take me to prison, you mean." Her breath shuddered out and she stared at her hands, as if she could still see Caine's blood on them.

"Just finish it out and tell me the rest. We'll figure out what happens next."

"I was so angry," she said, tightening her hands into fists. "I knew what Caine was saying was true. When Genny first came to speak to me she didn't tell me the details of what had happened and how John died. But I knew it was bad. That he'd done something wrong. And then Caine told me you were the one who killed him and I just went crazy. How could you do that? He was your friend.

"How could you!" Her hand cracked against Jack's cheek like a whip, and her elbow knocked her water glass over so it spilled across the table. She crumpled and her body shook with harsh sobs. The manager started to make his way across the restaurant to us, but the look on my face had him turning away.

I felt the waves of hurt coming from Jack and knew he blamed himself everyday for John's death. For not suspecting that he'd been dirty and for firing the shot that had ended his life, even though he'd had no choice. But he didn't defend himself to Jane. I didn't have any problem defending him. I didn't care what Jane Elliott had suffered. She didn't have the right to blame Jack for anything.

"Don't ever touch him again like that or I'll cut you in two," I said, my voice hoarse with anger. "Jack did what he had to do." I wasn't going to stand by and let him take the blame when he'd done nothing wrong. "He almost died that day too. And by your husband's hand."

"It's okay, Jaye—" Jack said, squeezing my thigh.

"No it's not, but I've made my point." I clamped my mouth shut before I said anything else I might regret.

"What happened next, Jane?"

"Andrew told me he would prove he was telling me the truth. That he had the documentation and that he was going to go to the FBI with the information. So he left me in the motel and told me he'd be back in an hour. I didn't know what else to do, so I called them. They told me I had to if anyone ever asked about the foundation. They said they owned me. They'd paid for me. And they said they could take it all away just as easily as they'd given. They never said it, but I knew that meant they'd kill us if we betrayed them. I had to protect my children."

She bowed her head and started crying again and Jack took my hand in his under the table. I was tired, and I wanted nothing more than to leave this place and never set eyes on Jane Elliott again. She was weak and a disgrace, and she was just as much to blame for the murders of Jack's men as anyone.

"Finish it out, Jane. Who did you call?"

She was resigned now as she answered. "I called Genny. She's my contact. There's a chain of command."

"Then what happened?"

"I relayed all the information that Caine had told me and that he was going to get proof. Genny hung up the phone and maybe fifteen minutes later I got another call. The woman didn't identify herself, but I could tell by the way she spoke that she was the one in charge. She knew things about me. Personal things that she wouldn't have known unless I'd been under surveillance."

"Do you have your phone on you now?" Jack asked. "Is it the same one you had then?"

Jane dug through her purse and held up the phone. "It's the same."

"It's possible we can trace the callers. It'll give us something besides circumstantial evidence."

She handed it over and Jack stuck it into his shirt pocket.

"What did she say to you?"

Her breath hitched again and quiet sobs shook her body. "She said that I had to kill him. Kill Andrew. I was still so angry and hurt by the things he'd said, and she played on that. She told me he was setting me up and that everyone would think that John died a traitor if I believed his lies. She told me that was all my girls would remember about their father, and she said the only reason Andrew had been sleeping with me was because he thought I was just as guilty as John and needed to get close to me to prove it. She said a man like him would never be interested in a woman like me otherwise.

"I—I believed her." Jane's eyes were drenched and searching, as if she wanted us to understand why she took a knife to a man. "And then she reminded me that the organization owned me and I had no choice but to do what she said or face the consequences. She said my girls had sure looked cute walking to school that morning. She even described what they'd been wearing." Another choked sob broke through and she covered her face with her hands.

"Andrew came back to the room a little while later with a legal size envelope full of papers. I told him I didn't need to see them. That I believed him and that I was sorry." She swiped the tears from her face and managed to look up at us, and her lips trembled as she tried to gather herself. "He told me he loved me and that he would protect me, but all I could think about was what would happen to my children if I didn't do what she said.

"Andrew always carried that big knife in his bag, and he'd left it in the room with me. So while he was gone I put it under the pillow and knew there was only one way to kill him. He was a big man, and I knew I couldn't overpower him. So I seduced him instead." Jane looked at her hands again like they didn't belong to her. They were fine boned, delicate, and smooth. Hardly the hands of a killer.

"So I did it." The words barely came out as a whisper. "I did it for my children and I live with the nightmares of the surprise in his eyes as he realized what was happening." She laid her head down on the table and her entire body shook as she wept.

"It's too late for all that now, Jane." Jack's voice was sharp, and I could feel the anger vibrating from him. He no longer felt sympathy for this woman—pity, yes—but not sympathy. "Who came to help you get cleaned up?"

Jane sat up but slumped in her seat, defeated. "I'm so sorry, Jack. Don't be angry with me. Please. I need your help."

"Then finish it out."

"I don't know who they were. I was so scared. In shock. And there was so much blood. It was everywhere. I got sick and had to run to the bathroom. All I could think about was getting the blood off. I climbed in the shower and turned the water on as hot as it would go, and then I just laid there as Andrew's blood washed down the drain."

Her voice was almost robotic now as she relayed the rest of the events. "Two women showed up out of nowhere. I don't know how they got in the motel room, but they were just there all of a sudden. They wore gray jumpsuits and they doused me in some kind of chemical. It got all the blood off, but it burned my skin. But not even the pain really got through to me.

"They cleaned the drains and used the same chemical on the bathroom to clean up all the blood and my handprints. They wrapped my hair in a protective cap and dressed me in a jumpsuit to match theirs. They put gloves on my hands and plastic booties on my feet, and then we went back into the room where Andrew was.

"It didn't even seem real. He just lay there on the bed, his eyes staring blankly at the ceiling. And God—the blood. I wanted to be sick again, but I wasn't. All I could do was stare at his body and try to come to the terms with the fact that I was the one who'd done that. I honestly don't even remember holding the knife. It's like it was someone else."

I shook my head in disbelief. When she went to trial she'd probably say that exact thing to give her a chance at diminished capacity. My anger was rising by the minute, and I wanted nothing more than to put my fist through something. But Jack rubbed the back of my hand with his thumb and I knew he wanted me to keep silent for just a little while longer while she got the rest of it out. I remembered then that Carver had asked Jack to keep his line open. She was making a full-recorded confession.

"They cleaned the knife and all the surrounding areas with the cleaner and then they planted strands of hair and other things on his body. I was told they paid off the office manager and a couple of vagrants across the street to say they'd seen Andrew go in the room with another woman. A blond prostitute. Witnesses came forward from a bar down the street and said they'd seen him leave with a woman who matched the same description as the one the manager and vagrants gave. These people have so much power. You understand now why I don't like to leave my house."

"Yeah, I understand."

I felt sick inside and I could only imagine how Jack felt. This was more than personal to him. "Did Andrew have a tattoo?" I asked her.

"Not by the time we started sleeping together. But there was a scar on his back, just above his shoulder blade where he said he'd had one removed. I knew it was the same one you all had. The one that matched John's. Andrew didn't want me to see it and remember John. Remember that they'd been as close as brothers once. So he had it removed. For me."

"Can you give me a description of the women who cleaned you up at the motel?"

Jane had control of herself now, as if confessing her sins had lifted a weight off her shoulders, and she trusted Jack when he said he'd help her. She was just about to answer when the front windows of the restaurant exploded. Shards of glass and wood flew toward us and people screamed as the air filled with acrid smoke.

20

"DOWN! DOWN!" JACK YELLED AS HE THREW ME BODILY TO the floor. "Try not to breathe and crawl back toward the kitchen."

My eyes watered from the tear gas and I started crawling while Jack covered me protectively. I looked back to see if Jane was behind us, but all I saw was smoke. Blood rushed in my ears so the screams and coughs of the other people were muted. My hands and knees bled as I crawled across broken glass, but I kept moving forward.

I coughed as we crawled through the swinging doors to the kitchen, but breathed in the fresh air as soon as it was available.

"Where's Jane?" I choked out. Tears streamed from my eyes, and I noticed Jack had his weapon out and trained at the door, though his eyes were red and watery as well.

"She didn't make it. A shot came in with the tear gas. It was long range and directed at Jane. Someone didn't want her to talk."

"Oh, my God." I realized then how close Jack had come to dying. If Tydell had been able to get a second shot off then Jack would be just as dead as Jane. He was a target, and nothing was going to stop these men until they'd met their goals.

The kitchen was in chaos. Food had been left on the stove and was burning in pots and pans. Dishes had been dropped and plates lay broken on the floor.

"We need to get out of here. The police will take care of the people out front. Tydell's shot hit its target, but they're not going to want to let me go since I'm already here and separated from my protection. Stay close behind me. Do you have your gun?"

"I've got it." I'd gotten in the habit of carrying it in my jacket pocket instead of my purse whenever I was out in public. I grabbed the gun and felt the weight of it in my hand. I wasn't sure how accurate I'd be because my eyes still watered and my vision was blurry, but it made me feel better to have it just in case.

Just in case happened before we made it to the kitchen door that led to the area where trucks unloaded the food. All I saw was a blur out of the corner of my eye right before Jack crashed into a rack of cookware with the weight of a man dressed in BDUs on top of him. Jack's gun skidded across the floor and my heart stopped as the other man pulled a knife long and sharp enough to cut to the bone with one slice. I knew without an introduction that I was looking at Lester Grimm. And he was here to kill us.

The man was heavier than Jack, but Jack managed to use his leverage to roll them across broken dishes and food. Metal shelving crashed down as they rolled. They moved too quickly. My gun was trained on them both, but they were so close together I couldn't risk taking a shot without hitting Jack too.

"Oh, God. Oh, God," I prayed over and over again. My eyes still watered and the two of them blurred together as Jack struggled to dislodge the knife from the man's hand. Their positions reversed again and Jack was on bottom. Both of his hands gripped around the wrist of the hand holding the knife, but it moved closer and closer to his neck, nicking the flesh so a thin stream of blood ran in a single rivulet. I didn't have any choice but to try and take a shot or Jack would die right in front of my eyes. And then I'd be next.

I used my shirt to blot my eyes and try to clear them a little, but it didn't help much. I decided to aim high and below the waist just in case my vision was worse off than I thought. I didn't think as I pulled the trigger. Couldn't think or I would've been paralyzed with the fear.

The gunshot echoed in the cavernous kitchen and I saw the man on top of Jack jerk slightly, but he didn't lose his focus on the task of cutting Jack's throat. I moved around to see if I could get a better angle and my eyes started watering again. Though this time it was with tears.

"Come on, Jaye." The pep talk wasn't working. My hand shook as I took aim again and I noticed the blood pooling beneath them from the wound in Grimm's leg. I was afraid to fire again and was glad I didn't when their bodies shifted and they rolled once more so Jack was on top. He slammed his elbow into Grimm's nose and I heard the sickening crunch of bone and cartilage, and then I winced as Jack's knee pressed into the man's groin.

An unearthly scream filled the air and brought chills to my arms, and the sound of gagging filled the room. Jack slammed the hand holding the knife against the floor and the man grunted as his wrist broke and the knife slid across the floor.

I ran over to the knife and kicked it farther away as Jack got up and picked up his gun, training it on Lester Grimm.

"You're under arrest. Roll over and place your hands behind your head. You have the right to remain silent." Jack finished reading his rights and cuffed Grimm's hands behind his back before he looked at me. "Nice shot, Tex."

"It's probably not a good time to tell you I wasn't really sure what I was shooting at. There was two of both of you." I still pointed my gun at Grimm and it weighed like lead in my shaking hands, so I put it back in my jacket pocket.

"Yeah, I probably could've gone without knowing that."

"You're bleeding."

Blood dripped down Jack's throat and stained the collar of his shirt, and I grabbed a dishtowel that was lying on the counter and went up to staunch the bleeding.

"I guess Lauren will be happy," I said to try and distract myself from the fact my hands were shaking. "You're bringing him in alive."

"Yeah, he's alive." He hissed out a breath as I blotted at the wound. "But I wouldn't feel too bad about it if he had an accident somewhere along the way."

"You don't need stitches. It's just a knick."

"Are you going to kiss it and make it better?"

I took his face between my hands and kissed him gently on the lips. "You scared me. Let's not do that again."

His arms wrapped around me and I buried my face against his chest. "If you want to know the truth I was pretty scared too. I'm probably going to need a lot of comforting later on."

"We'll comfort each other then."

21

A COUPLE OF HOURS LATER WE WERE ALL BACK INSIDE THE
Federal Building. We'd been seen to by the paramedics and
given clean clothes to change into. My body was starting to
feel the aches and pains of being knocked to the ground and
crawling through glass. I could only imagine how Jack felt.
I'd seen the bruises already starting to show themselves from
his run in with Grimm.

Jane Elliott had been the only casualty at the restaurant, the
result of a well-timed military strike. Jesse Tydell had made
the killing shot while Grimm had taken care of shooting the
tear gas canisters and cornering Jack to eliminate him. They'd
come close to eliminating one more name from their list. But
they hadn't succeeded, which meant they'd keep trying.

Jack and I were back in the same observation room we'd been
in the last time we were here. Lauren and Carver stood next
to us. As interrogation rooms went, I'd seen worse, but I was
hoping after today not to see another one for a long while.

Agent Greer sat across from Grimm, but Grimm slouched

back in his chair, ignoring Greer completely. His hands were handcuffed in front of him and his ankles were shackled. The shot to his leg had only been a flesh wound, so the paramedics had wrapped it up and sent him along with the FBI team that had arrived on scene. Grimm hadn't said a word, and he didn't look particularly worried to be there.

"You're in a lot of trouble, Grimm. Maybe you can help us out with a few things and the FBI will consider lightening the charges."

Grimm grunted but didn't say anything else.

"You're looking at two counts of first degree murder—the murders of two police officers and the attempted murder of another. Those are death penalty offenses. You're going to want to talk to us."

"I'm as good as dead anyway if I talk to you," he said, shrugging. "I'd just as soon have the lethal injection and go out the easy way. I've heard it's very humane."

Grimm smiled, showing small even teeth that seemed abnormally white against his skin. The look in his eyes made me shudder, and I wrapped my arms around myself in comfort. His gaze was empty—completely soulless—and he stared at Greer as if he knew everything about him. Almost like a dare.

Greer acted as if he were bored. "You were pretty high up in the Vagos. In charge of your own territory. And you had a shot at being General but you blew it. You got caught and Lassiter was killed. That leaves Jesse Tydell."

"He's the new General. It's his game now."

"Like I said, Grimm, we'll be willing to cut you a deal on some of the charges."

"You gotta prove I killed someone first." Grimm smiled again.

"Don't flatter yourself. You're not that smart. We've got your knife and we'll find blood on it that belongs to the victims. You're going to want to come clean before those tests come back. Once they do, the deals aren't going to be so good. Who paid you for the hits?"

Grimm played with the length of chain between his cuffed hands, clanking it against the arm of the chair. "Don't know," he shrugged. "Don't really care. The money showed up in the accounts when it was supposed to."

"How'd you get your orders?"

"It was all electronic. Like I said, money showed up in each of our accounts and we got emailed instructions. Tydell's good with the electronics, but he could never trace where it came from. Seed money showed up as a sign of good faith, but we didn't take the bait right off. You've got to be careful with stuff like that. It could've been the cops trying to smoke us out. So we asked for a sign of good faith in return."

"What kind of good faith?"

"I want immunity."

"It's not going to happen, Grimm. You killed two cops and tried to kill another. All I can do is lessen the sentence."

"I want a low security facility and visitation rights. A man like me would be king in prison."

"An attorney from the Department of Justice is waiting to talk to you after I finish here. You can take it all up with her. Now give me some information or I'm going to put you in a cell and throw away the key."

Grimm stared down Greer, but Greer didn't flinch. He just waited him out. When several minutes went by, Greer picked up his file and stood to leave.

"South Carolina is an electric chair state," Greer said as he opened the door to leave. "That's where you killed Detective Price. Don't think that's going to be an easier way to die than whatever your new General can do to you."

"Arnie Mays," Grimm said, before Greer could leave the room.

Greer closed the door and sat back down across from Grimm, and Carver opened his laptop beside me and ran the name through his database.

"What about Arnie Mays?" Greer asked.

"He was the sign of good faith."

"Got it," Carver said into the earpiece Greer was wearing. "Arnie Mays was a cop working out of the South Bronx before he got caught for corruption, bribery, and illegals. IAB has a full file on him. Mays went off the grid and was suspected of being swept up by the Vagos as a soldier. His body washed up in San Francisco last December."

"So they killed Arnie Mays. Why?" Greer asked. "He was one of your own."

"Mays was undercover. All that bullshit in the IAB files and the charges filed against him were all a set up. He slipped up and it was noticed. We've got too many ex-cops in our organization for a plant to not be caught. Mays managed to fly under the radar for more than ten years though. He was good. But we've got guys who are better. There was a reason Mays never warranted his own territory with that many years in. Why he was slow moving up the ranks. We never really trusted him."

"So as a sign of good faith, you asked whoever gave you the orders to show they were serious by taking Mays out of the game?"

Grimm shrugged, but the smirk on his face was admission enough.

"Thanks, Grimm. You've been very helpful." Greer left the interview room and a moment later he came inside the observation room.

"What's the status on Paris Spencer and Grace Lieber?" he asked.

"They're both en route," Lauren said. "About another hour or so."

"You going to try and shake them up a bit?" Jack asked. "Maybe they need to accidentally run into each other and see that the game is over."

"Exactly what I was thinking, Sheriff Lawson," Greer nodded. He turned to Lauren and said, "Go ahead and do what you need to do with Grimm and then call Agent Donaldson. Let's make sure Paris Spencer and Grace Lieber see each other on their way in. I also want them to catch sight of Lester Grimm. They would've done their homework, so they'll recognize who he is and wonder how much he told us. I want to see who rolls first. One of those women is guilty of ten counts of murder. The other is an accessory."

———

"THERE'S GOT to be someone else to do this," I said twenty minutes later. Jack had changed into a pair of black cargo pants and a black T-shirt that had been dug up from somewhere, and he ran his hands over the rifle in the case in front of him.

"I'm the best person for the job at the moment. I can shoot the long distances. I have the training."

"Only you don't work for the FBI and we're not in the same state where you're sheriff. Last time I checked, you need a badge for this sort of thing or you get arrested."

Carver came in at that exact moment and slapped a piece of paper on the table in front of Jack. "Sign here. You're authorized for temporary duty."

"Nice," I said, throwing up my hands in resignation. "If you're going up there, then I am too. And don't even try to argue about this with me."

Jack took the rifle from the long black case and methodically checked it. "This is the perfect opportunity to catch Jesse Tydell. We probably won't get another chance like it. We'll have Grimm, Lieber, and Spencer on the front steps of the Federal Building. Tydell will want to eliminate Grimm because he already knows he's had time to talk to us. Chances are he knows one of the women is the one giving him the kill orders. He's very intelligent, and our profilers say he wouldn't want to share any information he might find out on his quest to make General. He thinks he's calling the shots, and he's cleaning up loose ends."

"We'll have Grimm in a controlled environment," Carver

said. "This is on our terms. We're presenting him with the opportunity. Jack will be invisible on top of the Federal Building, and he'll have a perfect line of sight to all the buildings where Tydell might be hiding. All Jack has to do is spot him and let the teams know which building to block off."

"What happens if Tydell shoots before the teams can stop him?"

"Jack will stop him first. Lauren only needs one of the Vagos alive."

"You don't have to go up with me, Jaye. I'll be perfectly safe and it'll be over before you know it happened."

"I'm going up with you. If you can see Tydell through your scope that means he'll be able to see you too, if he's looking. It never hurts to have another pair of eyes."

Jack nodded and his lips twitched a little. He was having fun. "Grab a pair of binoculars from Carver. You can be my spotter."

––––––––

I FOUND myself on top of the Federal Building flat on my stomach, looking through the binoculars at the three buildings across the street that Tydell might be hiding in. The sun beat down overhead and my clothes melted into the rooftop while the back of my neck blistered.

"Are you sure he'd do something like this in the middle of the day?" I asked. "There are people everywhere. How's he going to go unnoticed?"

"He'll blend in. The buildings across the street are all businesses. He'll be wearing a suit and have a briefcase hiding his rifle. He'll have walked right in with the lunch crowd. He's already found his place and is set up. We've shut down all of the empty offices that have windows. He'll have to use the rooftop."

Sweat snaked down my back as I looked for movement on any of the rooftops. We only had a matter of minutes before Grimm, Spencer, and Lieber had their run in on the front steps. If we didn't find Tydell before that, someone was either going to die, or Tydell would be scared away for good.

"If it were you, where would you shoot from?" I asked Jack. I had no idea how he stayed still and focused for so long. All I could think about was the heat of the rooftop burning into my stomach and the dizzying height.

"The one on the far right. It'll be a harder shot for him to make, but that doesn't matter. He's good at what he does. It's the building that has the least security, and all of the angles of the roofline give good cover."

"The car with Lieber is just down the street," Greer said. I heard the drone of his voice through the listening device in Jack's ear. "Grimm's being brought out the front to the waiting police van at the curb so he can be taken to the courthouse for booking. You have a minute to find Tydell or this mission is aborted."

I swung the binoculars to the building Jack suggested and moved slowly across every peak and valley of the roof, the seconds ticking off in my mind.

"Come on, Jaye. Give me something."

"I'm trying, dammit. I don't see anything." And then I did.

Just a glint of the sun off a piece of glass or metal, but it was enough. "Got him." I relayed the information to Greer so they could have agents move into place.

"Give me the distance measurement from the lower corner of the binoculars."

I rattled it off, the adrenaline pumping through my veins as the seconds wound down, and I felt Jack make a tiny adjustment next to me. The shot wouldn't be easy to make. I could only see the side of Tydell's face and part of his arm.

I held my breath and watched through the binoculars as Jack pulled the trigger. The shot was loud and I heard people on the streets below screaming, but I kept my eyes trained on Tydell as the bullet made contact and he crumpled to the rooftop.

Chaos erupted below us, and I watched as agents swarmed from everywhere to contain the scene.

"You make a pretty good spotter, Doctor Graves."

"Maybe so, but I think I'd rather be up to my wrists in a chest cavity than ever have to do that again. Much less exciting."

"But now you have all that adrenaline to work off. I bet I could help you out with that."

"Jesus. Only a man could think of sex at a time like this." I was drenched in sweat, filthy from the rooftop, and sunburned.

"It's a special talent. Like a superpower."

"All I can say is that it's a really good thing I love you. But maybe we could have a shower first before you show me your superpowers."

22

WE STAYED THE NIGHT IN DC AND SPENT MOST OF THE NEXT day giving statements and signing official documents, so it was well after dark by the time we drove back to King George County. We rode in comfortable silence mostly, each of us lost in our own thoughts.

Having Paris Spencer and Grace Lieber see each other and Lester Grimm had worked out exactly as the FBI planned. They couldn't wait to turn on each other in hopes of a lighter sentence. Not that it would work. Murder was murder. And they were both going away for a lot of years.

But in the end it was Grace Lieber who had masterminded the entire scheme—forming the charities for funding, finding someone to commit the kills, and cold bloodedly deciding to end the lives of all the men who had taken her sons away from her. She wanted revenge and she'd have stopped at nothing to get it. She'd stated for the record that she'd gladly do it all again. Her only regret was she hadn't been able to see the contract fulfilled with Jack and Wolfe's death.

Paris Spencer had pleaded to lesser charges of accessory, fraud, and cybercrimes since she'd been handling the money and technology end of things. She'd do time, but it wouldn't be for a lifetime like Lieber.

I wasn't sure what was going to happen with Lester Grimm. Lauren had taken custody of him and whisked him away to the Department of Justice building. My only hope was they wouldn't put him back out on the street to gather information. I had a feeling a man like Grimm held grudges a long time, and I didn't always want to be looking over my shoulder. They'd need to keep a tight leash on him, and I hoped they didn't regret whatever deal they'd ended up making with him.

All in all, I was glad to be back in our small slice of the country. I'd had enough of the FBI and the city for the moment, and I was happier than I thought I'd be to get back to the slow life. Maybe I'd gotten used to it.

To my surprise, Jack had turned down another job offer with the FBI. He was going to take his vacation and then see what happened with the next election. He wasn't going to rush into anything and he wanted to take a break. I couldn't say I blamed him. I was looking forward to taking that break with him and spending some time together as a couple without the interference of crime scenes and bodies. We were being selfish. And it felt pretty damned good.

"We're getting married in a week," I said. It was really starting to hit me.

"That's the rumor going around. When I talked to mom this morning, she said she had everything taken care of. All we have to do is show up. And you need to find something to wear."

"It's a shame she can't do that part too. I've never been very good at picking out clothes."

"I don't think it really matters. They're all going to end up on the floor by the end of the night anyway. It's what you wear underneath that really matters."

I grinned and then something in the distance caught my eye. "What's that?" Brightly colored lights pulsed and flashed in the sky about a mile down the road.

"Looks like a carnival of some kind. Why don't we stop and check it out? I'm on vacation after all."

"As long as you buy me some cotton candy and try to kiss me on the Ferris wheel."

"I'm up to the challenge."

"You always are," I said, thinking of the night we'd spent together.

The streets were packed with cars and once we got through the gates it was nothing but wall-to-wall people. It seemed like everyone in the county had the same idea as us. We moved with the traffic, jostling back and forth as we made our way toward the Ferris wheel.

The hairs on the back of my neck stood up just before my father moved in front of us and stopped us in our tracks. I barely noticed the people who bumped into me from behind.

My dad wore shorts and a T-shirt and his head was covered with a baseball cap. He looked like everyone else enjoying their evening out.

He smiled like him showing up was an every day occurrence and he stuck his hands in his pockets. "I just wanted you to know I wish I could be at the wedding. It would be nice to walk you down the aisle."

Jack tensed beside me and I felt him shift as he reached for his gun and handcuffs.

"You're leaving?" I asked, wondering why I found the news so disappointing.

Jack made small movements and kept his gun down by his side so as not to cause panic around us. "I have to take you in, Malachi. Don't make this harder than it has to be. Turn around and put your hands on the back of your head."

My breath caught in my throat as Jack gave the order. My dad just smiled at Jack and didn't make any move to do what he'd been asked. Then he looked back at me with a twinkle in his eye.

"I just wanted to say goodbye, honey. And to tell you not to trust anyone. There's more going on here than meets the eye. I'll be back when I can. You two be good. And maybe think about giving me some grandchildren."

"Don't do this, Mal," Jack warned.

I knew my father was a wanted man—a criminal—but I didn't know how I'd feel if I had to watch the man I was going to marry arrest the man who had raised me. Fortunately, my father took the situation into his own hands.

My dad looked at Jack's gun and raised a brow, daring Jack to use it. Then he winked at me and disappeared back into the crowd as if he'd never been standing there.

"Son of a bitch." Jack put his gun away and started pushing

through the crowd, trying to follow behind him, but it was no use. Malachi Graves was gone. Again.

I grabbed onto the back of Jack's shirt so I didn't lose him too, and we finally made it back to the entrance. My chest hurt and my palms were sweaty at the thought we might catch him.

"You know I have to take him in, right Jaye? I don't have a choice in this," Jack said. He ran a hand through his hair, obviously frustrated, and he kicked at an empty popcorn bucket on the ground.

I sighed and tried not to let my relief show that my dad had escaped. "I know. I just wish it didn't have to be you."

"Unfortunately, I'm the only one who knows he's alive at the moment, so the task falls to me. Hurry and get to the car. Maybe we can get a road block set up before he slips through."

I caught him by the arm before he could start moving. Panic had settled somewhere in my stomach and I wasn't comfortable with the determination I was seeing on Jack's face. "You can't call this in, Jack. Not until we know the reasons why he had to fake his death. You told me how we handled this was my decision."

"And I stand by that. But he stood right in front of me. He's playing with us, wondering how far we'll go to catch him. You can't expect me to stand by while he does that."

"Yes, I can."

"Jesus, Jaye." He kicked the popcorn bucket again and then started moving toward the car. I knew he wouldn't betray my father. At least not yet.

I followed him back to the car, but I knew there was no point in searching for my father. We wouldn't find him. It was impossible to find ghosts.

I stopped when we got to where the car had been, and it took me a minute to process the fact that it wasn't there. An empty parking space was all that was left and there were no cars going in either direction on the street.

"Sometimes I really dislike your father," Jack said, standing beside me with his hands on his hips as he looked at the empty space.

My lips twitched once before a terrible thought struck me. "Oh, my God. The boxes! That's what he came back for all along. He wouldn't be saying goodbye if he didn't have them."

"They're locked in the safe inside the house, and up until a couple of hours ago Wolfe was there." Jack got on his phone and asked for a patrolman to come pick us up.

"Do you really think that will matter?" I asked once he disconnected.

Jack started to say something and then stopped as he thought it through. "Shit. We need to get back to the house. But you're probably right. I bet they're long gone."

We wasted precious minutes waiting to catch a ride, and we rode in tense silence all the way back to Bloody Mary. By the time the patrolman pulled into Jack's driveway, I knew for sure we wouldn't find the boxes in the safe. Jack's car was parked in the garage as if it had never been anywhere else.

Jack waved the patrolman away and then pulled his weapon. We entered the house, and I followed behind Jack while we checked each room for signs of my father. The house was empty. I didn't need to walk through it to know for sure.

We got to the top of the stairs and went into the master bedroom where the large walk-in safe was built into the closet. The safe door stood wide open. The cash, guns, and other valuables were exactly where they were supposed to be, but there was no sign of the boxes. In their place was the small circle of silver that had belonged to my mother. I picked up the ring and slipped it onto my right hand.

"Son of a bitch," Jack said. "I guess it's a good thing we were able to get a few of those flash drives to Carver. There must be something really important on there."

I twisted the metal around my finger, trying to figure out how I felt about all of this. "Did you ever think that maybe he was telling the truth? Maybe things aren't what they seem and we need to find out the truth. He said he'd be back."

Jack looked at me with pity and pulled me into his arms for a hug. "Babe, that's exactly what I'm worried about."

NEXT JJ GRAVES MYSTERY...

Grab the next novel in the J.J. Graves Mysteries...

Down and Dirty

Wedding plans are in full swing in Bloody Mary, Virginia. J.J. Graves is ready to walk down the aisle and start a new life—despite the fact her father is still on the loose, blood money is stashed in her closet, and an unidentified body is missing from her parents' bunker.

But it isn't her personal life that's threatening her chance to say "I Do." It's the remains of a brutally murdered corpse found buried beneath a prize-winning rose garden. And the message attached leaves no bones about it - the body is meant for J.J. The clock is ticking as J.J. and Jack search for a killer before he becomes the ultimate wedding crasher.

WHISKEY REBELLION

If you enjoyed DIRTY ROTTEN SCOUNDREL, you might enjoy WHISKEY REBELLION, the first book in Liliana Hart's Addison Holmes Mysteries!

I've made a lot of bad decisions in thirty years of living. Like when I was eight and I decided to run away from home with nothing more than the clothes on my back, peanut butter crackers and my pink Schwinn bicycle with a flat front tire. And the time when I was sixteen and decided it was a good idea to lose my virginity at an outdoor Metallica concert. And then there was the time I was nineteen and decided I could make it to Atlanta on a quarter tank of gas if I kept the air conditioner off.

There are other examples, but I won't bore you with the details.

Obviously my judgment has gotten worse as I've grown older, because those bad decisions were nothing compared to the one I was about to make.

"Hey, Queen of Denial, you're up."

I gave the bouncer guarding the stage entrance my haughtiest glare, sucked in my corseted stomach, tossed my head so the black wig I wore shifted uncomfortably on top of my scalp and flicked my cat-o-nine tails hard enough to leave a welt on my thigh. It was all in the attitude, and if I had anything to do with it, The Foxy Lady would never be the same after Addison Holmes made her debut.

The music overwhelmed my senses, and the bass pumped through my veins in time with the beat of my heart. The lights stung my eyes with their intensity, and I slunk across the stage Marlene Dietrich style in hopes that I wouldn't fall on my face. Marlene's the epitome of sexy in my mind, which should tell you a little something about me.

I'd run into a little problem lately, and let's just say that anyone who's ever said money can't buy happiness has obviously never had the need for money. My apartment had a date with a wrecking ball in sixty days, and there was this sweet little house in town I wanted to buy, but thus far the funds to buy it hadn't magically appeared in my bank account. I could probably make a respectable down payment in three or four years, but I had payments on a 350Z Roadster that were killing me, yoga classes, credit cards, a new satellite dish that fell through my roof last week, an underwear of the month club membership to pay for and wedding bills that were long past overdue. My bank account was stretched a little thin at the moment.

None of those things would be a big deal if I was making big executive dollars at some company where I had to wear pantyhose everyday. But I taught ninth grade world history at James Madison High School in Whiskey Bayou, Georgia, which meant I made slightly more than those guys who sat in the toll booths and looked at porn all day, and slightly less than the road crew guys who stood on the side of the highway in the orange vests and waved flags at oncoming traffic.

Since I'd rather have a bikini wax immediately followed by a salt scrub than have to move home with my mother, I'd declared myself officially desperate. And desperation led to all kinds of things that would haunt a person come Judgment Day—like stripping to my skivvies in front of men who were almost as desperate as I was.

The beat of the music coursed through my body as I twirled and gyrated. The lights baked my skin and sweat poured down my face from their heat. Something tickled my cheek. I caught a glimpse of black out of the corner of my eye and realized a false eyelash one of the working girls had stuck on me earlier sat like a third eyebrow on my glistening skin. I swiped at it nonchalantly, but it wouldn't budge. I ducked my head and peeled it off my cheek, but then it stuck to my finger and I couldn't get the little devil off.

I shimmied down to my knees and knelt in front of a portly man with rosy cheeks and glazed eyes that spoke of too much alcohol. His sausage-like fingers came a little too close, so I gave him a slap with my whip to remind him of his manners and the fact he was wearing a wedding ring.

I ran my fingers through his thick, black hair and left the eyelash as a souvenir of his visit to The Foxy Lady. The thought crossed my mind that he might have a hard time explaining the eyelash to his wife, but the music kicked up in tempo and I had to figure out something else to do with my remaining two minutes on stage. Who'd have guessed it would take me thirty seconds to run through all my dance moves?

The arches of my feet were screaming and I almost laughed in relief when I saw the poles on the far side of the stage. I could spin a few times and hang upside down a few seconds to take the pressure off my feet. Besides, I watch T.V. Men always seem to go crazy for the pole dancers.

My sweaty hand clasped the cold metal pole and I swung around with more gusto than was probably wise. Little black spots started clouding my vision, so I slowed my momentum down until I was walking around like a horse in a paddock on a lead rope.

I made another lap and saw Mr. Dupres, the club's owner, frowning at me. He swung his arms out and gestured something that resembled either taking off his shirt or ripping open his chest cavity, and I realized I still had on every scrap of clothing I'd walked on stage with. I threw my whip down with determination and ripped my bustier off to reveal the sparkly pasties underneath. I tossed the bustier into the audience and cringed as it knocked over a full drink into some guy's lap. Just call me the human version of a cold shower. Not a great endorsement for a stripper. I waved a little apology in his direction and tried to put a little more wiggle into my hips to make up for the mishap.

Would this freaking song ever end?

I prayed someone from the audience would have mercy and just shoot me. I spun one last time on the pole and nearly fell to the ground when I saw a familiar face in the audience.

I would have recognized the comb-over and pasty complexion anywhere, though when I usually saw Principal

Butler he didn't have a stripper grinding in his lap. I kind of hoped the way his glasses were fogged would keep him from seeing me, but when he took them off and wiped them on his tie my hopes were dashed. He did a double take and blinked like an owl before he paled.

I just wanted to vomit.

Mr. Butler practically shoved the woman in his lap to the ground and reached for something in his pocket. He pulled out his cell phone and snapped off a picture. Not good. I guess he wanted proof to show to the school board before he fired me.

I covered myself with my arm and edged back toward the curtain. The music pounded. I waved to a few customers on the front row, their faces twisted and disgruntled at my early departure. I considered my bounty. A grand total of seventy-two cents on a bed of peanut shells lay at my feet.

Tough crowd.

Principal Butler's eyes were still glued to my chest as I finally found my way behind the thick curtains at the back of the stage. It was a darned good thing there was only a week left until school was out. Maybe the summer would give Mr. Butler time to forget he saw me in pasties and a thong and me time to forget that I saw my principal's tiny excuse for an erection.

Or maybe not.

————

So it turns out I'm not cut out to be an exotic dancer, and I'll be checking the employment section of the paper again.

I had to say that after the conversation I just had when I was fired from The Foxy Lady, I probably couldn't count on them to give me a glowing recommendation.

"Listen, Addison, I just don't think you're cut out for this type of work," Girard Dupres told me after my first and only routine.

I can't even begin to tell you how many times in my life I've heard those exact words. If I weren't such a positive person, I would live in a constant state of depression.

Anyway, Mr. Dupres was the guy who hired me, and he looked like a Soprano's reject—thinning dark hair, beady eyes, hairy knuckles and greasy skin. He obviously didn't know anything about hiring good strippers or he never would have considered me.

I decided it was best to look slightly downtrodden at my termination, but inside I was relieved that exotic dancing wasn't my calling. I don't think I pulled off the reaction I was hoping for, because Mr. Dupres thought it would be a good idea for me to perfect my technique in a private showing just for him. But to give him the benefit of the doubt, it's hard to have a conversation and not look desperate when you're topless and covered in sweat.

I told Mr. Dupres "Thanks, but no thanks," and headed back-stage to gather my things and get dressed. I decided to keep the costume and cat o' nine tails just in case I ever had a dominance emergency, but I left the itchy wig on the little plastic head I'd borrowed it from.

I took out the blue contacts I'd worn to cover my dark brown eyes and creamed off the heavy eye makeup. I pulled my dark hair back into a ponytail, slipped on my jeans and baby-doll tee from the Gap and stepped into a pair of bright pink flip-flops. It was nice to see the real Addison Holmes once again. I'd only misplaced myself for a few minutes, but it was long enough to make me realize I liked the real me enough to find some other way to make the extra money I needed.

I'd just hide this little incident away and no one but Mr. Butler and me would ever know about it.

I pushed open the heavy metal door that led from the dressing areas to the alley behind The Foxy Lady and squinted my eyes as the sun and heat bore down on me. I slipped on a pair of Oakley's and hitched my bag up, digging at the bottom for my car keys.

If I'd been looking where I was going instead of at the bottom of my purse, I'd never have tripped over the body. I'd probably have walked a wide path around it and wondered how someone could already be drunk enough on a Saturday afternoon to be passed out in a strip club's parking lot. As it was, my foot caught the man right in the ribs and sent me sprawling to my hands and knees.

"Ouch, dammit."

I muttered various curses as the raw skin on my palms bled. I pushed myself up slowly and took stock of my aching body. My jeans had holes in both knees and a lot of blood covered the toes of my right foot.

"What the hell?" I said as I wiggled my toes to see what the damage was. There didn't seem to be any cuts so I turned around to see what I'd fallen over.

The body sprawled out in the gap between the cars. It seemed twisted in an odd arc, but shadow shielded me from witnessing the carnage that created so much blood. If nothing else, I knew where the blood on my toes had come from. I couldn't pretend he was drunk with the dark stain spreading out across his dress shirt like a Target ad. Nor would I be able to keep my recent dabbling into the exotic arts a secret once I called the police and explained to them I'd just found my principal dead in the parking lot.

ABOUT THE AUTHOR

Liliana Hart is a *New York Times*, *USA Today*, and Publisher's Weekly bestselling author of more than sixty titles. After starting her first novel her freshman year of college, she immediately became addicted to writing and knew she'd found what she was meant to do with her life. She has no idea why she majored in music.

Since publishing in June 2011, Liliana has sold more than six-million books. All three of her series have made multiple appearances on the New York Times list.

Liliana can almost always be found at her computer writing,

hauling five kids to various activities, or spending time with her husband. She calls Texas home.

If you enjoyed reading *this*, I would appreciate it if you would help others enjoy this book, too.

Lend it. This e-book is lending-enabled, so please, share it with a friend.

Recommend it. Please help other readers find this book by recommending it to friends, readers' groups and discussion boards.

Review it. Please tell other readers why you liked this book by reviewing. If you do write a review, please send me an email at lilianahartauthor@gmail.com, or visit me at http://www.lilianahart.com.

Connect with me online:
www.lilianahart.com
lilianahartauthor@gmail.com

ALSO BY LILIANA HART

The MacKenzies of Montana

Dane's Return

Thomas's Vow

Riley's Sanctuary

Cooper's Promise

Grant's Christmas Wish

The MacKenzies Boxset

MacKenzie Security Series

Seduction and Sapphires

Shadows and Silk

Secrets and Satin

Sins and Scarlet Lace

Sizzle

Crave

Trouble Maker

Scorch

MacKenzie Security Omnibus 1

MacKenzie Security Omnibus 2

Lawmen of Surrender (MacKenzies-1001 Dark Nights)

1001 Dark Nights: Captured in Surrender

1001 Dark Nights: The Promise of Surrender

Sweet Surrender

Dawn of Surrender

The MacKenzie World (read in any order)

Trouble Maker

Bullet Proof

Deep Trouble

Delta Rescue

Desire and Ice

Rush

Spies and Stilettos

Wicked Hot

Hot Witness

Avenged

Never Surrender

JJ Graves Mystery Series

Dirty Little Secrets

A Dirty Shame

Dirty Rotten Scoundrel

Down and Dirty

Dirty Deeds

Dirty Laundry

Dirty Money

Addison Holmes Mystery Series

Whiskey Rebellion

Whiskey Sour

Whiskey For Breakfast

Whiskey, You're The Devil

Whiskey on the Rocks

Whiskey Tango Foxtrot

Whiskey and Gunpowder

The Gravediggers

The Darkest Corner

Gone to Dust

Say No More

Stand Alone Titles

Breath of Fire

Kill Shot

Catch Me If You Can

All About Eve

Paradise Disguised

Island Home

The Witching Hour

Books by Liliana Hart and Scott Silverii
The Harley and Davidson Mystery Series

The Farmer's Slaughter

A Tisket a Casket

I Saw Mommy Killing Santa Claus

Get Your Murder Running

Deceased and Desist

Malice In Wonderland

Tequila Mockingbird

Gone With the Sin

Made in the USA
Coppell, TX
17 June 2021

57651408R00164